THE LIGHTHOUSE MURDERS

Richard Baldwin

© Buttonwood Press 2007

This novel is a product of the author's imagination.
The events described in this story never occurred. Though localities, buildings,
and businesses may exist, liberties were taken with their actual location and
description. This story has no purpose other than to entertain the reader.

Published by Buttonwood Press
P.O. Box 716
Haslett, Michigan 48840
www.buttonwoodpress.com

ISBN: 978-0-9742920-5-2

Printed in the United States of America

This book is dedicated with love, to my sister,
Gayle Howard Baldwin Brink of Dallas, Texas.

Gayle and I grew up in Grand Haven, Michigan
where we enjoyed many days at the beach with friends.
The lighthouse beacon and the fog horn were constant
reminders of our home on the shore of Lake Michigan.
In adulthood, Gayle, her husband Dick, children Mac
and Abby, along with their spouses and children enjoy
summer visits to their beloved Nestlewood, one of
many cottages bordering the shore of the Great Lake.

Gayle has always been one of my biggest fans,
and I, one of hers.

OTHER BOOKS
BY RICHARD L. BALDWIN

FICTION:

A Lesson Plan for Murder (1998)
ISBN: 0-9660685-0-5. Buttonwood Press.

The Principal Cause of Death (1999)
ISBN: 0-9660685-2-1. Buttonwood Press.

Administration Can Be Murder (2000)
ISBN: 0-9660685-4-8. Buttonwood Press.

Buried Secrets of Bois Blanc: Murder in the Straits of Mackinac (2001)
ISBN: 0-9660685-5-6. Buttonwood Press.

The Marina Murders (2003)
ISBN: 0-9660685-7-2. Buttonwood Press.

A Final Crossing: Murder on the S.S. Badger (2004)
ISBN: 0-9742920-2-8. Buttonwood Press.

Poaching Man and Beast: Murder in the North Woods (2006)
ISBN: 0-9742920-3-6. Buttonwood Press.

The Searing Mysteries: Three in One (2001)
ISBN: 0-9660685-6-4. Buttonwood Press.

Ghostly Links (2004)
ISBN: 0-9660685-8-0. Buttonwood Press.

The Moon Beach Mysteries (2003)

ISBN: 0-9660685-9-9. Buttonwood Press.

The Detective Company (2004; written with Sandie Jones.)

ISBN: 0-9742920-0-1. Buttonwood Press.

Unity and the Children (2000)

ISBN: 0-9660685-3-X. Buttonwood Press.

NON-FICTION:

If A Child Picked A Flower Just For You (2004)

Buttonwood Press

The Piano Recital (1999)

ISBN: 0-9660685-1-3. Buttonwood Press.

A Story to Tell: Special Education in Michigan's Upper Peninsula 1902-1975 (1994)

ISBN: 932212-77-8. Lake Superior Press.

Warriors and Special Olympics: The Wertz Warrior Story (2006)

ISBN: 0-9742920-4-4. Buttonwood Press, LLC.

ACKNOWLEDGEMENTS

I wish to thank Buttonwood Press Editor Anne Ordiway for her advice and guidance in telling a good story. I also wish to thank Buttonwood Press Proofreader, Joyce Wagner, who is meticulous beyond reason; and Sarah Thomas, Buttonwood Press Graphic Designer, for aiding me and the reader with a professional presentation of the story. Others who offered technical assistance include: Ann Liming, Suzette Cooley-Sanborn, Jerry and Barb Roach, Mrs. Bell and her students at Greenville High School, Mindy Wilson, John Tromp, Jack Kelly, Kate VanAllsburg, Linda Clymer, and Bob Cavera.

The lighthouse featured on the front cover of this book is the Squaw Island Light, in the middle of Lake Michigan. The photo, as well as those on the back cover, is used with permission from Jerry Roach, photographer and author of *The Ultimate Guide to West Michigan Lighthouses*.

INTRODUCTION

The real names of lighthouses have been used in this novel. In reference to those lighthouses, nothing except the names of the lighthouses and their locations is real. To find out interesting and true information about these unique lighthouses as well as all Great Lakes Lighthouses, readers are directed to three books by Photographer and Author, Jerry Roach. The books are titled, *The Ultimate Guide to West Michigan Lighthouses; The Ultimate Guide to East Michigan Lighthouses,* and *The Ultimate Guide to Upper Michigan Lighthouses.* The books can be purchased at www.lighthousecentral.com or by calling 810-938-3800.

I hope you enjoy this story, set in a beautiful part of America, the Great Lakes.

One more thing: for readers of my previous books, with this mystery I add a new assistant, Jack Kelly. I hope you enjoy this character, because he is one.

— *Richard L. Baldwin*

The Pharisees asked Jesus why his disciples were allowed to eat with unclean hands, violating a long tradition of the Jewish faith. Jesus responded that they were missing the point. "It is what comes out of a man that makes him unclean. For it is from within, from men's hearts, that evil intentions emerge: fornication, theft, murder, adultery, avarice, malice, deceit, indecency, envy, slander, pride, folly. All these evil things come from within and make a man unclean." — Mark 7:21-23

So, it is with this mystery. As this story unfolds it is the evil within a number of hearts that leads to acts that most of us find reprehensible. Detective Lou Searing and his new assistant, Jack Kelly, endeavor to unearth the consequences of evil to bring justice to people.

Every mystery story has a problem, a conflict, a dastardly deed to mess up the works, and I won't let you down. Such is the case in this story which begins in the den of a wealthy gentleman in southeast Michigan…

Arthur S. Webberson had asked his family to gather in his den at eight o'clock the evening of June 10 for an important meeting having to do with his last will and testament. Curious family members cancelled conflicting commitments to be present. With a light rain falling on Gloucester Lane in exclusive Bloomfield Hills, Michigan, Arthur entered his den and politely greeted his wife Florence; his son Wallace and daughter-in-law Beatrice; and his daughter Victoria and her husband Bertrand Wilkshire. Finally, in the den was Arthur's 73-year-old brother, Theodore, who had exhausted all of his savings and investments and was now penniless and living in a group home where administrators quickly snatched his Social Security check when it arrived in the mail.

When Arthur, age 65, entered the room, everyone rose. He wore a fashionable suit, with a tie that did not match; the tie sported a picture of the Big Sable Point Lighthouse. Arthur had a ruddy complexion, bushy eyebrows, a rather large nose, and he wore a monocle.

Ted had a hard time getting up. After rising, he let out a loud belch, much to the displeasure of all present. Victoria, his niece, thought it was inadvertent, the result of a man not in control of his actions. Wally didn't say a word but he would have bet his last dime that his uncle wanted simply to announce Arthur's arrival.

Ted hadn't had a haircut in months. He was dressed in wrinkled trousers because he wore the same pair for weeks at a time. He was wearing a well-worn white shirt and a red-on-black polka dot bow tie that snapped onto the collar. Ted glanced often at a crossword puzzle he held precariously in his lap, along with a magnifier.

Florence was formally dressed and, while waving her light hanky from side to side near her face, rose and came to her husband's side. She leaned near his ear and whispered, "I beg you one more time not to talk about your plans to disperse your estate. The implications will be disastrous. I know what I am talking about, Arthur." Arthur nodded to indicate that he had heard Florence but had no intent to follow her suggestion. He motioned for her to be seated.

Arthur sat in a large wine-colored leather chair behind a huge walnut desk. "Thank you for coming," Arthur began, as if welcoming stockholders to an annual meeting. "I have decided to explain how my fortune is to be dispersed when I leave this world, a happening some of you wish for daily, and an event others hope will never come. But, come it will, perhaps sooner than any of us think."

Wally took Bea's hand and gave it a squeeze. Victoria seemed to tear up a bit and brought her frayed and damp tissue up to her eyes. Theodore seemed to smile, but most would have been surprised if old Ted understood a word.

Arthur continued, "Rather than have my attorney, Mr. Scott, bring you together to explain the will, I have decided to satisfy your curiosity and tell you what will happen to my estate.

"At the moment, or rather I should say at the closing bell of the New York Stock Exchange, my estate was worth two hundred million dollars, give or take a few million. I expect its continued growth; but even if I should die tonight, these are my wishes regarding what will happen to the money."

Everyone in the room sat straighter, not wanting to miss a word; Arthur might have been about to announce the winner in the Mega Bucks Lottery.

Enjoying their undivided attention, except for Theodore who looked a bit confused, Arthur began. "To my beloved, Florence: you have your own estate, and you have sufficient money to provide for your every need, even if you live a long life. So, nothing in my estate shall transfer to yours."

Wally smiled and thought, The old man won't even give Mom a dime; but all the more for me. Once again he squeezed Bea's hand as if to say, Make some plans to spend a lot of money.

Florence lowered her head and sighed. Her exclusion was no surprise, for Arthur had made his intentions clear before bringing the family together. She, unlike the others, knew where all his money had come from, and while she was disappointed in Arthur's decision, she silently wished that he would give her something.

"To my brother, Ted: at your age and with your current care and Social Security, I see no reason for you coming into money. So, I will leave you one thousand dollars, which will be earmarked for the pine casket you always wanted. You can't say your wealthy little brother never did anything for you, Ted."

Most in the room thought Ted didn't understand, but perhaps he did; he sat up, looked at Arthur, slowly raised his right hand, touched the tip of his thumb to his nose and waved his hand. Victoria gasped, drawing Ted's attention. Their eyes locked, Ted winked, and then smiled for the first time in several months.

With two relatives remaining and only one thousand dollars designated, Arthur's son and daughter sat in quiet anticipation. "To my daughter Victoria and her husband Bertrand: I leave ten million dollars. Victoria, my most precious child, and the joy of my life — you always took time for Daddy, didn't you, sweetheart?"

Victoria, dressed in a black business suit, her silky true blond hair in an unfashionable bun, nodded and smiled.

"Oh, thank you, Daddy. You needn't, really, Daddy." Bertrand, with visions of a BMW swirling in his head, quickly responded to his wife's willingness to give the money back by speaking up loudly, "Thank you, thank you, thank you, Mr. Webberson. You are most kind, sir."

"Yes, I am, and I only ask that Victoria do something for me in return."

"Oh, yes, Daddy. I'll do whatever you want."

"Thank you, Vicky. All I ask is your love." Arthur smiled and put a check next to Victoria's name.

"Five letter word for 'harass'," bellowed Ted. Everyone started, but no one responded, thinking that Ted simply didn't have the mental capacity to understand the seriousness of the moment.

"This leaves my son Wallace." Wally's heart raced in anticipation of a fortune; he was ready for a huge gift. "To my son Wally, I bequeath twenty million dollars." Wally slowly rose and hugged not his father, but his mother, and then his wife, Bea.

"There is one condition, however," Arthur continued, as his audience seemed to freeze in anticipation.

"With you, there is always a condition," Wally snapped, pointing a nervous finger like an imaginary pistol at his father, and shouting, "You'll go to my football game, if… You'll come to my recital, if… You'll be at graduation, if… Before we all hear the big IF with this gift, I've had it with you and your conditional 'IFs.' I'd rather have been born to a pauper, and been loved, than to have been sired by a selfish, greedy controlling tyrant."

Arthur wasn't surprised by his son's outburst. In fact, it was predictable. Arthur took a deep breath, and delivered the big IF.

"The twenty-million was to be yours, Wallace, if you treated me with the respect a father deserves. We have all seen in your predictable immature explosion that you won't, so the twenty million stays where it belongs — in my estate." Everyone squirmed in his or her seat, and as if on cue, let out a collective sigh. Victoria, who shortly before had felt overcome with joy at a gift of ten million, belatedly wondered why her prodigal brother should get twice her gift. What had she done to be so mistreated by her father? Within a couple of minutes, Victoria's attitude changed from grateful to humiliated.

Wally defiantly took Bea's hand, rose, and dragged her from the room. Once they reached the living room, Bea's fury erupted. "For once, just once, Wally, couldn't you simply say, 'Thank you, Father,' and shut up?" Bea paced back and forth, shaking her head with a grimace and tight face.

"I don't want his dirty money!" Wally replied in a sharp tone of voice.

"Twenty million dollars, Wally — twenty million. All you had to say were two words, 'Thank you'." Bea continued to pace. "Ninety-nine percent of the world would kiss your father's feet if he gave them twenty million dollars. But you — you chose this moment to snap at his generosity, and in an instant, neither of us has a cent. Honestly, Wally, your behavior is disgusting!"

"Relax," Wally replied. "I'll apologize. I always do, and he always hugs me and gives me what I desire. We haven't lost anything. Dad and I were just playing out our father-and-son roles."

In the den, Mr. Webberson continued. "With the return of Wallace's twenty million to the estate, that leaves about one hundred eighty-nine million, nine hundred ninety-nine thousand," Arthur said quietly. "I hereby bequeath that balance of my account to the Huron, Ontario, Michigan, Erie, Superior (HOMES) Lighthouse Association. They can renovate some lighthouses and assure the preservation of these beacons of hope for generations to come."

This announcement didn't come as a surprise, but it did cause everyone, including Ted to take a deep breath and shake their heads from side to side.

"Are you sure you want to do that with your money, Daddy?" Victoria asked.

"Oh, yes. Your children will be sufficiently cared for and they can be resourceful in amassing their own fortunes."

"How about giving me the money you had earmarked for Wally?" Victoria suggested. "As you said, I always took time for you. I'm not ungrateful for the small inheritance, but since Wally won't be getting it, and, as far as you were concerned, it was spent, perhaps you could bring my inheritance up to thirty million?"

Theodore smiled, recognizing this demonstration of sibling rivalry as another in a litany of spats between Wally and Victoria; they had spent their lives challenging one another for Arthur's love and attention.

"Ten million is what I bequeath to you, my dear Victoria. I know that the Lighthouse Association can really use the money and it will be well spent. So, I'll just revise these papers and we'll have my will wrapped up by Mr. Scott and his associates. Thank you for coming.

"And speaking of legal counsel, when I die, all procedures related to my remains, interment, cremation, funeral or memorial service will be dictated by Mr. Scott who has been given a full description of my wishes. None of you will have any say in any of this, relieving you of concern of what I would want. It also assures me there will be no family conflicts about any after-death dealings with my body or my estate."

Arthur stood up, and as he exited the room, the remaining family members rose and nodded in respect. Ted didn't rise but he bellowed, "Anybody know a seven-letter word for 'tyrant'?"

Florence, who had followed Arthur out of the den, interrupted, "I really think you are making a huge mistake. I ask that you please stop this nonsense."

"Giving my money to the Lighthouse Association is nonsense? That group has offered me more love and attention than everyone in that room combined, and you know it!" Arthur exclaimed, pointing to his den.

"Calm down, you fool!" Florence retorted. "Family is family. Take care of them, for crying out loud; take care of them before you take care of bricks and mortar and a bunch of outdated buildings that have been rendered useless!"

"My dear Florence," Arthur said indignantly, "for the last time, I will say that the money in my estate was earned and carefully invested by me; not Ted, not Victoria, not Wally, nor you. It is my money, and I can do with it as I wish. I gave Ted a decent pine casket. I gave Victoria a wonderful gift. I gave our first-born and only son twenty million — and was I thanked? No, I was verbally abused.

"I love lighthouses and I love the people who enjoy them. And, yes, as hard as it may be for me to say this and for you to hear it, I love the association and its members more than I love my own family. So, I am giving my inheritance to my family, not blood relatives, but to those who share my love for our Great Lakes heritage, and to those who love the open waters and the ships that plied them. Now, if you and my ungrateful family will excuse me, I will call Mr. Scott to take the necessary steps to make this will a legal document." With that, Arthur turned and walked away leaving Florence alone with her advice being unappreciated.

Florence found Wally in the library. Bea had stepped outside for a cigarette. "I love you with all of my heart, Wally, but you sure said the wrong thing at the wrong time."

"Yeah, I know. I'll talk to Dad; patch it up like I always do. He'll give me the twenty mil."

"I don't think so," Florence replied. "Not this time. His mind is made up and other than his gift to Victoria, and his token gift to Ted; you're not getting anything."

"You mean I'm out of the will — totally cut out?"

"I'm afraid so."

"I can't believe it," Wally said, realizing for the first time that the money wouldn't come his way. "What's he going to do with it? Give it to that Homey Lighthouse Association, or whatever it is called?"

"Absolutely. He loves the HOMES Lighthouse Association more than he loves me or you or Victoria."

"Well, I don't need millions from Dad. Your inheritance will be all I need."

Florence paused, took a deep breath and replied, "Don't count on that, Wally."

"What's that supposed to mean?" Wally asked, shocked at his mother's words.

"I was raised to believe that each person in the family needs to create his own million and to receive it on a platter is no honor. My parents didn't leave me a thing, and I worked hard to earn and invest every dollar. I expect you, if you want money, to do the same. Your father and I have given you an education, but you'll have to make your fortune on your own."

"I expected you to help me get my designer clothes business off the ground," Wally countered loudly. "That'll take thousands. I expected, at the least, a little help, Mother. Is there no privilege in being a Webberson?"

"I am not going to repeat myself, Wallace. You need to grow up and handle your own business. There will be no inheritance from me, and as a result of your immaturity in confronting your father, none will come from him either."

"You can't be serious," Wally said, almost in a state of shock.

"I am serious, Wallace. I love you, but let me remind you that love has nothing to do with money, a concept that you can't comprehend right now. I hope in time that you'll understand what I have been trying to teach you since you were a child." Wally stormed out of the library, found Bea, and the two quickly left.

The driver of a ride service for the disabled signaled the security officer to be let into the Webberson estate. The gate opened, and the van-like vehicle slowly made its way to the front door. Ted was helped into the accessible van in his wheelchair, with his ever-present crossword puzzle on his lap, and thirty minutes later arrived at his group home. He was helped into the house by an attendant. Inside, three men in wheelchairs and one on the sofa sat watching *Law and Order*.

Ted liked all the men in the home, but Ike was a real buddy. Ike, too, had once wielded power, handled millions, and then was forced to use all his resources to treat and care for the disease that racked his body. The two were soul mates, sharing memories, crossword puzzles, and regularly enjoying television game shows.

Ted had nicknamed his friend after President and General Dwight D. Eisenhower. Ike wasn't a wheelchair user; in fact, he was quite mobile and able to leave the home, often for a few days at a time. He was not as poor as Ted, but he did need help managing his money. Unlike Ted, Ike had no family to visit him or to show concern for his well-being.

Interrupting a dramatic scene in the TV show, Ted said to Ike, "Kid brother of mine told the family how he was dishing out his money tonight."

"Are you going to be a millionaire, Ted? Is that it?" Ike asked with a smile, trying to attend to the TV and his friend.

"Nah. He gave me a thousand bucks to get a pine casket and a few nails. A thousand bucks hardly pays for the handles on a casket these days. I'd rather he had given me a thousand dollars' worth of crossword puzzles. Imagine that, a thousand bucks for a funeral."

"You two need to move to Philadelphia and get a little brotherly love," Ike replied, distracted by the television.

"It's too late for that."

"Aw, Ted, it's never too late for patching-up, you know that," Ike replied, offering a spiritual solution to a family disagreement.

"Nope, too late," Ted said. "He's giving all his millions to a lighthouse association. Imagine that, Ike. He's giving his millions to a bunch of people who stand around gawking at useless buildings!"

"I have to agree with you there, Ted. It's hard to understand." By now, all of Ike's attention was on their conversation. "Are you going to challenge the will, or get a little revenge?" Ike asked, rubbing his hands together in anticipation of a conflict.

"I might. At our age, we could use a little excitement around here. Are you with me, Ike?"

"You get a plan, and I'll be your man."

"Ok, it's a deal. What's a six letter word for hindsight?"

"Wisdom."

"Thanks."

2

Wally was incensed at what he perceived to be his father's cruelty. There had been conditional love, there was no question about that. But always, there had been forgiveness, a getting back to normal; enough that Wally had thought his father would never leave him out of his will.

Another reason for his shock was that Wally knew a secret about his father, and Arthur knew that Wally knew it. The last thing Arthur Webberson would want was for his son to reveal the secret. Yet by writing his son out of the will, he practically assured its exposure.

While Arthur expected that the revelation would be forthcoming, Wally was taking steps to get his revenge. If he couldn't have the money, he would make sure that the association wouldn't either. Not only that, but his father would learn a big lesson in conditional love.

The next morning Wally called his attorney Winston Ellerby to explain the situation and to seek advice on what approach to take. He had also decided to tell him his father's secret so that the attorney could factor the information into whatever advice he might offer.

"Dad has a special skeleton in his closet," Wallace began. "He would never want it to become public. I think I can use this information to extract an inheritatnce that is rightfully mine."

"Whatever you share with me, Wallace, stays with me," Winston replied. "You know that."

"Yes, I do, and that is why I am willing to tell you. My father was married before," Wally began. "And he had two children. He left his wife, walked out the door when his children were four and two, and never returned. My father never looked back, and to my knowledge, never had contact with his wife or children since the day he left them in Lima, Ohio."

"What was his wife's name in Ohio?"

"Abigail Dickenson."

"I take it Abigail took no legal action when her husband deserted the family?" Winston asked.

"She didn't know where he'd gone. He went to California, met and married my mother. They soon moved to Michigan where he made his millions supplying parts to the auto companies. Victoria and I were both born and raised in Michigan."

"Arthur's name change — when did that happen?"

"After my mother and father met in California, he went from Dickenson back to Webberson. He took his first wife's last name when they married in Ohio, and I think I heard that this first wife never knew his surname."

"That's odd," Winston said.

"He's odd — always has been, always will be," Wally said, shaking his head.

"Wallace, this is interesting, but it's hardly shocking, or of a nature to keep this a secret."

"Except that Abigail committed suicide. His children, adults at the time she did this, vowed to find their father and sue him for years of neglect. My father believes that if these two adult children ever find him, he could lose his entire estate."

"I see," he paused. "Do you know anything about these two adult children?"

"Oh, yes," Wally offered. "I know a lot about them and believe me, my father has every right to fear discovery. But I am fairly certain they don't know about Victoria and me."

"Well, you should consider teaming up with them in seeking the estate as his legal children."

"This is your advice?" Wally asked.

"No, just thinking aloud. But you'd be hard-pressed to find a judge or jury who wouldn't lean toward awarding a man's wealth to his own blood, especially if your half-brother and half-sister are struggling financially. Are they?"

"No, they are not."

"Then, why would they want to go after his money if they don't need it?"

"They want his land."

"He didn't figure his land into his estate?" Winston asked.

"Oh no, Father is only talking about stocks and bonds — his real assets are not considered part of his inheritance. Ever play Monopoly?" Wally asked.

"Oh, sure."

"Let's just say, he's got a lot of hotels on the board!"

"What would become of his real estate upon his death?" Winston asked.

"This leads me to the rest of his secret. His land is supposed to go to a mistress who lives in London."

"You're making all of this up, Wallace," Winston said, shaking his head. "This certainly can't be in your father's past."

"The power of money is vast, my friend," Wally said with a smile. "This mistress isn't some peasant in a foreign land. She is a minor member of the royal family."

"Queen Elizabeth?" Winston asked, now believing that anything was possible.

"Not quite," Wally chuckled. "I won't reveal her name, but the National Enquirer would pay me more for the story than I might have received from my father's estate."

"This could explain why he is announcing his intention at this point," Winston replied. "It's not common to summon the family and explain the future distribution of wealth. He may be leaking this information to get his legal papers in order, preparing for any challenge from these two older children or the mistress, whoever she may be."

"You could be right."

"Another question, if I may. What are the children's names?"

"My half-brother's name is Arnold Dickenson. My half-sister's name is Alice Dickenson Livernois." Winston paused while he wrote down the names.

"Does Victoria know what you know?"

"Absolutely not."

"How about Florence?"

"Not a chance!"

"Theodore?"

"Maybe. Many years ago Ted and Dad were close. I wouldn't be surprised if Ted knew, but his mind is very bad now. Most of the family thinks he lives in another world."

"How do you know about this secret?" Winston asked.

"Dad took me to London when I was sixteen," Wally began. "He thought I had gone on a two-hour Gray Line Tour of London, but I didn't have enough money, so I went back to our hotel room. While I was pretty naïve at the time, I knew that what I saw when I walked in was something I was not meant to see. Dad sat me right down and told me in no uncertain terms that I must never tell anyone what I'd seen. If I did tell, Dad said he would deny it, and find some way to severely punish me."

"Ok, but how did you hear about your half-brother and half-sister?"

"That night, Dad drank heavily, and finally said, 'Wallace, you might as well hear the whole story.' He told me he hated his first wife and couldn't bear the thought of living with the witch, as he called her, and the kids were driving him nuts, so he packed a grip and went to California, didn't even leave a note."

"Then he told you their names?"

"That's right. I had a pretty good memory but I wrote the names down the first chance I got. Many years later I looked the two up — found them still living in Lima. Both became extremely wealthy and were living as dignified, upstanding citizens. The hospital is named after Arnold and the library is named after Alice."

"But, you didn't meet them. Correct?"

"Oh, no. I just went to Lima and played detective," Wally replied.

"Interesting. But, why would they care about any more land when they themselves are so wealthy?" Winston asked.

"Well, as I said earlier, if you knew the amount of land Dad owns, you'd understand. I've told you enough of my father's past. You have enough information to advise me, though there's more to the story."

"Wallace, I do have some immediate advice. It is absolutely essential that your father continue to live. If he dies, you'll lose bargaining power, because Probate and a slew of lawyers will be playing the cards while you stand by, practically helpless. So, if you have any thoughts of causing his demise because of what he's done, forget them right now. To get a share of the estate, we need your father alive. Do you understand?"

Wally nodded, but a good observer might have noted that the advice went in one ear and out the other.

3

Alice Livernois had an appointment with her attorney LeRoy Otterbee for their quarterly chat regarding her estate. Alice was overweight but she carried it well, was smartly attired, and was quite attractive with only a hint of grey hair. Her miniature dachshund, Roscoe, was always at her side or in her arms. Many people found this most inappropriate, but Alice adored the little creature and doted on it ad nauseum.

A quarterly meeting was as important to Alice as a monthly checkup was for a heart patient at the Cleveland Clinic. After reading and noting something in the margins of legal-looking documents, LeRoy declared, "Well, I think your estate is up-to date. Your stock selections allow for stability, with a healthy percentage allocated for growth, so your financial planner has done a good job. Is there anything else we need to talk about?"

"Have you ever done any private investigating?" Alice asked.

"Excuse me?"

"Detective work. Have you ever been hired to find someone, or to discover facts about another person?"

"Can't say as I have. That's not what I trained to do, nor has anyone asked me to get involved in anything like that," LeRoy replied. "Why do you ask?"

"I'd like to find my father. You can hire it out or do it yourself, but I want to find him."

"I must say I'm intrigued, but I'm never seen myself as a private investigator, as exciting as that may seem," Mr. Otterbee replied. "Why this interest in finding him?"

"He left my mother, my brother, and me when I was two. Maybe it's curiosity. Maybe it's a need to know what happened to him. Maybe it's time for revenge."

"Revenge?"

"He hurt many people, LeRoy. Karma is about to catch up with him, but I need to find him first."

"What do you know about him?" LeRoy asked.

"Practically nothing. Mother said he simply left, didn't leave a note, and never contacted her again."

"That's it? You don't know where he went, his name, anything?" LeRoy asked.

"Well, yes, his name is on my birth certificate. He is Arthur Dickenson and if he's still living, he's sixty-five. He was born in England. Beyond that, I know nothing."

"Did your mother ever talk about him?"

"Never in a positive way. She made it clear we should never ask."

"Did your mother ever remarry?"

"No."

"Is she still living?" LeRoy asked.

"No. She took her life — depression."

"While I do want to help you Alice, I must ask what kind of financial incentive there would be for me?" LeRoy said, seeing dollar bills fluttering before his eyes.

"How about an all-or-nothing proposition?" Alice asked. "If you find him, five million dollars. If you don't, you receive nothing beyond the most basic expenses — phone, document copying, and travel."

"Guess you've heard about the power of motivation," LeRoy said with a smile.

"My terms also indicate how much I want to find this man," Alice replied, looking LeRoy in the eye.

"I'll get right to work," LeRoy said, wondering where to start in finding Arthur Dickenson. With Roscoe under her arm, Alice left the office and entered her limo through the door held open by a uniformed driver.

Rose and Mary McCracken, twin sisters, had recently retired from careers at Alma College in Alma, Michigan. Rose was a professor emeritus in music, and Mary was a maintenance worker with forty years of experience. Two sisters couldn't have been further from one another on the bell curve. Rose had studied at the Juilliard School of Music in New York City. She had perfect pitch, could play the piano by ear, and was a child prodigy practically born to play Rachmaninoff's "Concerto in D Minor." She became quite well-known in music circles.

Mary was mentally impaired. Most psychologists compared her mental functioning to that of a nine or ten-year-old. She struggled in school, long before special education was common. An elementary custodian, Suzette Cooley, took Mary under her wing, teaching her general maintenance skills, and she actually found the work fun. Suzette would give her fifty cents every day she helped her. Mary used the money to buy records of her favorite country music singers. After fourth grade, Mary's parents removed her from school.

After Rose left home, Mary continued to live with her parents in Alma. Her father worked for Gratiot County, and her mother was a cook at the college. On the twins' 40th birthday, their parents were killed in an automobile accident, victims of a drunk driver traveling at a high rate of speed. Rose immediately left her concert tour and returned to Alma. She got a job in the music department and cared for Mary.

The twins, seeking an interest that would get them out of the house and away from their small mid-Michigan town, discovered lighthouse tours. Because they went on so many tours, always together, they became known to fellow lighthouse buffs as RoseMary.

Rose had dreamed of having her own lighthouse for decades, spending hours researching the purchase of a lighthouse and asking assistance from developers, realtors, attorneys, and even state and federal officials. At each turn she learned that Arthur Webberson held claim to the property, blocking her from realizing her dream.

Rose desperately wanted a lighthouse for herself and Mary. Rose planned to give tours, open a small shop, and spend weeks at a time reading mysteries and walking along the sandy beach. But whenever she inquired, she heard the same thing. "The light is not for sale. Should it ever be for sale, Mr. Webberson has staked a claim to the property." When she went to the General Services Administration, the government agency that oversees the most non-privately-owned lighthouses, she was met with a negative response. Her congressman investigated and learned the same thing: When he challenged the legality of such arrangements, he found everything was above-board. Arthur S. Webberson was powerful and influential and took great pride in his grip on available lighthouses.

Rose was sure that the only way she could acquire a lighthouse on the Great Lakes was either to break into the Webberson machine or to destroy it. If she destroyed Webberson's hold, she would need intelligence enough to make sure her name or actions never raised suspicion.

4

JUNE 20 · BAILEY'S HARBOR, WISCONSIN

St. Mary of the Lake Catholic Church was hosting an Elderhostel titled, *The History of Lighthouses in the Great Lakes.* The enrollees had taken a day trip along the shores of Lake Michigan and Green Bay to visit and explore unique lighthouses in Door County.

The Elderhostel guests were staying at the Blacksmith Inn. Often a renowned speaker was invited to address the group. In the evening, some of the attendees were too tired to listen to a lecture and went to bed early, but usually a good crowd was on hand because this was a rare opportunity to listen to experts talk about lighthouses.

Arthur Webberson was in the audience pursuing his aim to learn all he could about lighthouses. Hearing a distinguished speaker was definitely an opportunity that couldn't be missed.

Frieda Bowman, The Elderhostel hostess and tour guide with the HOMES Lighthouse Association, stepped up to the lectern. She was a take-charge, clip-board-under-her arm, middle-aged woman with stylish eye glasses resting on the end of her nose. Frieda lived alone, but was rarely home, spending much of her time on lighthouse tours. When most had focused attention on her, Frieda began. "Our speaker this evening is Dr. Leonard Wilkenson, one of the world's leading authorities on lighthouses. He has visited them in over a dozen countries and has written three books, including the widely-acclaimed

They Guide the Ships Through Storm and Peril. He is currently about half-way through a tour of the United States. Please give a warm welcome to Dr. Leonard Wilkenson."

Following warm and sustained applause, Frieda sat down at the end of the dais so she could see the Power Point presentation, the highlight of Dr. Wilkenson's talk.

"Thank you, Miss Bowman," began Dr. Wilkenson. He stood tall with a full head of pure white hair, a clean-shaven face, and eyes that seemed to penetrate the hearts and souls of his listeners. He enjoyed an instant rapport with his audience. Dr. Wilkenson's presence lent an air of sophistication to the man, given his formal attire, slight British accent, and delightful smile that seemed warm and genuine.

Dr. Wilkenson continued, "It is a pleasure to be with all of you this evening. The lighthouses of the Great Lakes are among the world's most beautiful because of their individuality, not only in their design, but in their settings. As Miss Bowman mentioned, I have traveled the world in search of lighthouses, and I can say with a great deal of certainty that the most unique lighthouses are right in the Great Lakes area. I am also pleased to note that one of your benefactors, Mr. Arthur Webberson, is in the audience. We owe him a debt of gratitude for all he has done, and continues to do, for those who love the lights." A round of applause followed. Arthur stood, smiled, and acknowledged Dr. Wilkenson.

"As many of you know, the lighthouses in the Great Lakes were built in the 19th century, at a time when shipping became a mainstay of the economy. Ships then did not have the sophisticated technology they have today. I doubt there was a mariner who even dreamed of what we know today as satellite positioning systems. Nor was radar a feature of ships when lighthouses began to dot the landscape.

"Before I present my formal program, I must tell you that a murder occurred almost one hundred years ago, at a light northeast of

Munising, Michigan, now called the Grand Island Old North Light. According to records, in the spring of 1905, the assistant keeper of that light, Derrick Morrison, was supposedly murdered by the keeper, George Gentry. When people went to the light to tell Mr. Gentry that his assistant's body had been found in a boat twenty-seven miles from the light, they found the light deserted. The keeper was gone and was never heard from again. This is a rare but tragic event in the history of the lights, but I offer this true story because the lights have witnessed ghosts, crimes, life-saving sagas, songs, and stories that make them a most interesting piece of Americana.

"This first slide is the lighthouse on Charity Island near the thumb of Michigan's Lower Peninsula, positioned at the entrance to Saginaw Bay. As you can see, it is in ruins. It is publicly-owned and the Arenac County Historical Society is attempting to renovate the structure."

A hand shot up in the front row.

"Question? Yes, sir," Leonard gave his attention to a tall, thin, elderly man, with long silver hair, a full beard and a moustache that was almost yellow from years of pipe-smoking. He looked like a hobo who had stepped into a meeting of distinguished-looking people.

"Thank you. You mentioned a lighthouse murder. Where was that again?" the man asked, cocking an ear toward the speaker.

"Grand Island Old North Light, near Munising in Michigan's Upper Peninsula," replied Dr. Wilkenson.

"Thank you. Do you know a story from around 1925, about a ship full of gold which sank off Squaw Island?"

"No, I don't believe so." Leonard became concerned that he had lost his audience and that this odd-looking old man would begin his own lecture.

"Supposedly a couple of men were able to take the gold from the sunken ship. Don't ask me how. That was before scuba gear and so forth. Anyway, they got that gold and then buried it near where the Squaw Island Lighthouse still stands.

"The lighthouse keeper went to bury his dead dog, so the legend goes, and hit upon this treasure chest of gold. Anyway, the guys that buried it there found out that the lighthouse keeper claimed it, and well, they, or one of the men, outright murdered the keeper to get the gold back. Never underestimate the power of greed. I think the murderer was from Beaver Island.

"Years later, it was believed that…"

"Excuse me!" Miss Bowman rose, interrupting the older gentleman. "Your story is interesting, but we're here to listen to Dr. Wilkenson, and time is getting away from us. If you don't mind, let's return to the lecture."

"I'm sorry. I thought my story was interesting and it relates to a lighthouse."

"Sir, are you registered for this conference?" Frieda asked, implying that the old man shouldn't be there.

"I most certainly am. You're questioning my right to be here? Is that what you're doing?" the old man asked indignantly.

"This is the time for our guest to speak. It's not a time for people in the audience to relate stories from the past. Do you understand?" Frieda shot back.

"How dare you humiliate me! If I have an interesting story to tell, I'll tell it, and I don't need any interruptions from you. Am I clear?" The people in the audience immediately felt great discomfort, not sure what might happen. A few quietly left the room in case the man became violent.

Dr. Wilkenson tried to calm the gentleman so he could proceed with his talk. "Thank you for sharing your story. I will gladly talk with you following the lecture. Would that be acceptable? I very much want to hear what you have to say."

"That's fine. Thank you. She'll pay for this. Understand?" He turned toward Frieda, "You don't embarrass me like this in front of people and not expect a payback." Frieda felt adrenaline flow into her bloodstream and realized that the odd gentleman, with a terrible temper who never before posed any problem, was now someone to be reckoned with.

At the intermission, Arthur Webberson sought out the gentleman who had offered the legend.

"That was an interesting story you told," Arthur said, standing in line for a cookie and some iced tea.

"Thank you. My name is Elmer Edwards, and my grandfather Lawrence Edwards was the man who was murdered. I didn't get to relay that because that rude woman cut me off. I didn't think that was polite."

"I thought she could have been a bit more tactful, yes," Arthur replied. "I'm sorry you lost your grandfather in such a terrible way."

"Oh, no sympathies are necessary. I never knew him, and maybe he had it coming for not giving the gold back. It certainly wasn't his, after all."

"Yes, but how could he know that it really belonged to the men who claimed it?"

"You got me."

☐☐☐☐☐

Early the next morning, the final day of the symposium, Arthur sought out Mr. Edwards.

"Good morning. Sleep well?" Arthur asked, making conversation.

"No, I didn't. Never do when I'm away from home."

"I'm sorry," Arthur replied. "My problem is getting my mind quiet enough to get to sleep. Once I relax, I'm OK."

"You're lucky," Elmer said. "And, be thankful."

"I am. How can I get any more information about your family and the murder of your grandfather?"

"Actually, my daughter has sort of taken this on. She wants to get to the bottom of it, so she's gotten quite a bit of information. To be honest, she's really into it for the gold."

"How can I reach her?" Arthur asked.

"I'll give you her phone number — or would you prefer her e-mail address?"

"Phone number is fine. What's her name?"

"Ruth Botsford. Her number in Portland, Oregon, is area code 724-555-9472."

"Thanks. I'll say hello to her for you."

"OK. You'd better wait a couple of hours. It's four a.m. there right now."

"Oh, sure. Let me ask: when the lighthouse was being built, why didn't the owner of the gold get the treasure out of the area? I mean it could have been found by the laborers."

"You got me again. All I know is that my grandfather was murdered, and he was a keeper at the Squaw Island Light. And as I said, he found a chest of gold that supposedly came from a shipwreck."

"Is there any more to the legend?" Arthur asked.

"The story most people accept is that a couple of sailors, the only survivors of the shipwreck, knew the cargo was gold, and they were able to get back to the sunken ship and retrieve it."

"Hmmm, interesting," Arthur replied, writing notes on his steno pad.

"This is oral history," Elmer replied. "You know that, I'm sure. There was no newspaper report — no radio, no TV, just word-of-mouth, and the passing from generation to generation of stories of the ancestors."

"I'll bet there is a lot of truth to the story, though," replied Arthur.

"We think so. You see, my father, who was seventeen at the time, saw it happen. He felt guilty all his life for not trying to help his father, but he was terrified. He didn't tell anyone that his father was murdered until just before he died. He was afraid the murderer would find him and kill him too."

"That's sad, living with fear all your life," Arthur said. "I wonder where all that gold is today."

"Its location is known," Elmer admitted. "It is not buried on a beach somewhere."

Arthur called Oregon about 8:30 a.m. local time.

"Hello. I'm calling for a Ruth Botsford."

"I'm Ruth Botsford. Who's calling?"

"My name is Arthur Webberson, from Michigan. I talked to your father a few hours ago at a lighthouse conference in Door County, Wisconsin. He tells me that you were quite interested in solving the murder of your great grandfather."

"That's right. For some reason, I'm quite curious about it. Guess I want the truth, and to know who killed him."

"Well, I understand there's gold to be found, also."

"That's my understanding," Ruth replied. "Why are you interested in this?"

"My passion is lighthouses," Arthur said with pride. "I love them and the people who enjoy them. Any information I can get is important to me. I have a few writer friends who thought it would make an interesting story, but I wanted to talk to you first to see if you think you have enough information to fill a book."

"Yes, it would probably fill a book."

"I assume you know where the gold is?" Arthur asked.

"As a matter of fact I do, but it's a family secret."

"Oh, I'm not expecting you to reveal any information. I was just wondering and nosy enough to ask if you had found it."

"Well, I have, but its location will stay only with me. Once I bring it up in public, you'll hear all about it. The media will simply eat this up."

"Yes, I imagine they will. Thanks for talking with me, Mrs. Botsford."

"You're welcome. Enjoy your lighthouses, Mr. Webberson."

Arthur hung up and then logged onto the Internet. He went to www.whitepages.com and typed in Botsford, Portland, Oregon.

A "search" brought up four names, including the phone number he had just called. Now he knew where Ruth Botsford lived and consequently where he could find the gold when she was encouraged to explain where it was being kept.

When the lighthouse conference broke for lunch, Arthur sought out Elmer and once again began a conversation. "Your daughter — the one with information about Squaw Island — does she have a family?"

"She lives with her son Robert, who is severely disabled — can't communicate without amazing technology, so she's with him twenty-four seven. I've tried to talk her into to finding respite care so she can travel and get some relief, but she won't hear of it. A mother has to do what a mother has to do, I guess."

"I understand. Her home is in Portland?"

"Small farm south of Portland, but it's a Portland address. Pretty place. I've been there a couple of times. I guess if you need to be in one place all your life, she's in a pretty place."

"She goes to town shopping, I assume," Arthur asked.

"Oh, yeah, she does get around. Neighbor lady watches Robert. But, she won't be gone overnight. The boy needs care."

"Well, she must be a fine woman."

"I think so, but then I'm a little biased."

"Has the conference been to your liking?" Arthur asked, deliberately changing the subject.

"You bet. Other than that rude hostess, I've enjoyed it. The best part is being around other people who like the lights. We're kind of a big family."

"Yes, I feel the same way," Arthur replied. "Nice meeting and talking with you. Maybe I'll see you at another conference or tour down the road."

"I reckon so."

Once Arthur learned that Ruth was the mother of a son with a significant disability, he lost all interest in obtaining the gold. For all his ruthlessness, he had compassion for parents who raise children with a disability.

Ruth got a call from her father.

"This is a 'heads-up' call, honey. I gave your name and phone number to a man at the Lighthouse Elderhostel I am attending in Wisconsin."

"Yes, I know. He already called."

"That was fast. He must be hungry for information."

"What is his name again? He told me, but I didn't note it."

"His name is Arthur Webberson. He's probably the best friend of the lights in the Great Lakes."

"He wanted to know about the gold. I figured he wanted to steal it from me."

"Oh, no, the man has more money than he knows what to do with."

"He said he had a friend who might want to write a book based on the story."

"That sounds like Arthur. Anything to bring attention to lights is something he would want to do."

"I told him I knew where the gold was, but I wouldn't tell him."

"I'm sure he is fine with that. Well guess my 'heads-up' is a little late."

"Thanks for calling, Dad. Love you."

"Bye, Ruth."

┌─────┐
│ 5 │
└─────┘

It was Tuesday, July 3, the day Jenny Mitchell came to visit members of the group home. Ted liked Jenny because she was smart. And Jenny didn't particularly like all the small talk with the other residents. With Ted, she could have an intelligent conversation. Often Ted would save the crossword puzzle clues he couldn't figure out for Jenny, and every time, Jenny would know the answer. Sometimes the two of them would sit together for more than an hour working on a crossword puzzle or discussing philosophy, politics, or world events. Ted had told Ike that if he had been about fifty years younger, he would definitely ask her out, or at least invite her to share a milkshake at the corner drugstore.

Jenny was 26, a graduate student at Eastern Michigan University in Ypsilanti, studying to become a social worker. She liked working with elderly people. Jenny was not exactly what one would call attractive. She could be the poster girl for what immature boys would say to one another, "Nothing to look at, but a nice personality."

That Tuesday afternoon, just before Jenny was to leave, Ted said something that would change both of their lives forever. "Do you remember telling me once that if there was ever anything I wanted, to tell you, and you would do it or get it?"

"Sure do. I meant it, too," Jenny said nodding her head. "Why, do you have something in mind?"

"Yes, but I don't think you'll want to do it," Ted replied.

"Oh, you'd be surprised at what I'd do," Jenny said with a smile. "I've liked you from the minute I started coming here. What do you want, Ted?"

"I want you to kill my brother," Ted said matter-of-factly.

"Ok," Jenny said calmly. "Just a few simple questions to get started; when, how, and where is he?"

"Really? You'd really kill my brother?" Ted asked surprised at Jenny's lack of emotion.

"Listen. I told you I'd do whatever you asked me to do. Why would I start putting limits on those requests? If this makes you happy, it makes me happy. Now, answer my questions. When, how, and where is he?"

"Sometime in the future, poisoning, and Bloomfield Hills. You'll find his address in the phone book," Ted shot back.

"Ok, consider it done," Jenny promised. "See you next week, Ted."

"I'll have more crossword questions for you, Jenny."

"I'll have a dead brother for you, Ted." Jenny smiled, then bent over and gave Ted a hug. She walked out to her car and drove away. She could add another three hours to her practicum log for her Senior Issues course at Eastern Michigan University. She had also hit upon a title for her Master's thesis: "Sibling Rivalry and Geriatrics."

Jenny would like to think that she was smart enough not to put herself in the position of murderer, but she knew that when she left Ted, he felt better, and that was what mattered. In her course on diseases of the elderly, she had learned that eventually people lose their sense of reality and often wander in a fantasy world. She was sure that Ted had simply expressed deep-seated hostility toward his brother. His idea of killing him was pure fantasy, and she would do what her professor said to do in these situations — accept the comment and move on.

The gavel came down hard on the solid oak table. "The meeting is called to order."

The Board of Directors for the Huron, Ontario, Michigan, Erie, and Superior (HOMES) Lighthouse Association was holding its annual meeting in the comfort of the Bay Yacht Club in Mount Clemens, Michigan. Most of the members were simple folk, interested in preserving a part of Michigan's past, and many felt a bit uncomfortable walking on the grounds of such a famous yacht club usually reserved for the very rich.

"I have brought you together to read a letter I received recently, instead of sending all of you an e-mail or a fax or even a letter," President of the Board Julian Hicks, tried to hold back a smile. "I did so selfishly so I can share in your reaction, something I could not do through an impersonal piece of correspondence." Julian's comments caused great curiosity, and the ten board members gave him their full attention.

"The letter, received from Attorney William Scott reads in part,

Mr. Arthur S. Webberson has directed that the bulk of his estate go to the HOMES Lighthouse Association. As you know, Mr. Webberson is most fond of the association, its members, and its mission. I am pleased to inform you that, upon the death of Mr. Webberson, the association will inherit a sum valued at more than one hundred eighty-nine million dollars. I ask your legal representa-

tives to correspond with me, so that, at the appropriate time, this transaction can take place quickly and without probate proceedings. Signed, William Scott of the firm, Scott, Nicholas, Benjamin, Jackson, and Weston, P.C. in Bloomfield Hills, Michigan.

Before Julian could put the letter down, the ten-member board broke into applause. They rose to hug one another. Presently wait staff brought in bottles of champagne. Corks popped and toasts were offered to Arthur and to the future good health of the HOMES Association. Finally, someone started to sing, "For he's a jolly good fellow…" and the mood was festive.

Once the din subsided, the members began to discuss among themselves how the association might use this inheritance; purchase lighthouses, restore lights — the list was limited only by a lack of imagination.

Julian brought the gavel down again, "The board members will kindly take their seats." The ten sat down and looked to their leader, who obviously had an agenda.

"I knew this news would be music to your ears." The members smiled and nodded, looking at each other happily. "I don't want to douse your enthusiasm, but there are a couple of things we need to consider. The first is that the family may contest this will. Arthur has a son, a daughter, and a wife. I have learned that only the daughter will receive a bequest, and by most of our standards, it will be a pot of gold at the end of the rainbow. Court action is certainly a possibility.

"The second is that the money will only come to our association upon the death of Mr. Webberson."

"How old is he now?" Norman Root asked.

"According to our membership data, Arthur is sixty-five."

"When did his parents die?" Norman asked. The other board members seemed surprised by his inappropriate question.

"I have no idea," Julian replied. "Why do you ask, Norman?"

"I'm trying to figure out when this money might come to us. With good genes, he could be around longer than our association."

"I understand your thoughts, Norman, but for the moment I think it best that we simply be thankful for this marvelous gift and enjoy Arthur for as long as he lives," Julian replied.

Norman leaned over and whispered to fellow board member Sally Windsand, "We sure could use that money now. If he wants us to have it, he should have given it to us outright. I don't like the idea of waiting for him to die. His getting hit by a MACK truck sure would help keep us in the black."

"Don't be talking like that, Norman," Sally hissed back. The two then gave their attention to Julian, who had moved on to other new business.

Five minutes later Norman wrote on his tablet for Sally to see, "Going to do what I can to bring that money to us real soon." Sally shook her head in disgust.

The Fourth of July vacationers in Manistee were either at the beach or walking downtown. The digital time-and-temperature display outside the Fifth Third Bank flashed 90 degrees. With no wind and high humidity, tourists and local folk window-shopped and took occasional refuge in an air-conditioned store. The Book Mark, long a favorite spot in Manistee, was one such store. Most people enjoy looking at the current best-sellers and browsing in their favorite genre for new books by their favorite authors.

A flyer taped to the door of the Book Mark announced the arrival of Michigan mystery writer, Lou Searing, aka, Richard L. Baldwin. "*Poaching Man and Beast* is finally out, folks, and you can get an autographed copy here at the Book Mark. Meet and talk with Lou Searing, Saturday, July 3, ten a.m. to noon."

Inside, the store's manager, Pat Sagala, was taking phone calls, arranging books, and keeping an eye on customer traffic. Pat supported authors and gave each the opportunity to sell a book or two, or maybe even experience the embarrassing situation of having no one appear at a book signing. This was not the case for Lou Searing, who was popular with summer tourists, especially those in the Manistee area. He was known because of a case he termed the *Marina Murders,* and in Ludington, he had solved the mystery he dubbed,

A Final Crossing: Murder on the S.S. Badger, a car ferry that traversed Lake Michigan from Ludington to Manitowoc, Wisconsin.

Lou is 65 years young, six-feet tall, has inherited male-patterned baldness, and wears two hearing aids to improve his hearing, damaged from measles at age two. He has a passion for driving a Harley Davidson and also owns several shares of stock in the company. His wife Carol is not a fan of his private detecting. Lou has been shot twice in the cause of solving six murders, and Carol doesn't want to lose the man she loves.

Lou and Carol have two children, Scott and Amanda, both married and raising eight beautiful grandchildren between them in Grand Rapids, Michigan, and St. Louis, Missouri. The Searings live in a beautiful home in the dunes south of Grand Haven. Carol's quilting studio and Lou's writing studio are on the second floor and both have marvelous views of Lake Michigan.

For the past ten years, Lou has combined his skill of solving hideous crimes with a joy of writing. "Solve it and write it," seems to be his motto. While Lou is solving and writing, Carol is volunteering, quilting, and bringing joy to the Searing's eight grandchildren.

Pat had set up an attractive display of Lou's mysteries, past and present, with a table and some chairs in front. Book signings were fun — handshakes, hugs, conversation, autographs, and happy customers. People liked the chance to talk to an author, get a personalized copy of a book, and shake the hand of someone who had accomplished what most only dream of doing.

Several minutes before the book signing was scheduled to begin, Pat approached Lou. "I've got a customer who wants to beat the crowd and talk to you for a minute or two," Pat said.

"Fine. Let's get this underway," Lou replied, walking toward his chair with stacks of books to his left and right.

"Lou, this is Doris Bouchet," Pat said. "She was here last year, had her picture taken with you, and she wants a book."

"Hi, Doris, nice to see you again," Lou greeted his first visitor. "Are you ready for another mystery?"

"Oh, yes. And, from what I've been hearing, your next case is right here in Manistee."

"Well, I never know where the next case will be, Doris. Crime never takes a holiday, or so they say. As you know, the marina murders began here in Manistee, but I doubt another murder will occur here. Lightning rarely strikes twice in the same place."

"You haven't been hearing the sirens?" Doris asked with a slight French accent.

"Oh, sure," Lou replied. "Could be anything — police, ambulance, fire."

"Two out of three isn't bad, Lou," Doris said with a smile.

"Two out of three what?" Lou asked confused.

"Police and ambulance. They're down at the pier. A body has been found at the end of the catwalk, next to the lighthouse. Word is that it's murder."

"Hmmm, no, I hadn't heard about that," Lou said, pleased to see the line begin to grow for his signing, but not happy to hear of the situation at the pier. If Mrs. Bouchet was right, his good friend Manistee Chief of Police Mickey McFadden was smack-dab in the middle of another mess.

"Well, unless it is a ghost story, you've got business to attend to," Doris said. Customers overheard the news and started the rumor that Lou wouldn't be around much longer.

The phone rang in the bookstore. Store employee Peggy took the call. A few seconds later she interrupted, bringing a portable phone.

"Lou, this is for you — Chief McFadden."

"Hi, Chief. According to a book-buyer, you are deep in a murder," Lou said.

"Hi, Lou. I heard you were at the Book Mark. If you don't have a line of your fans, I sure could use a hand. The Coast Guard has jurisdiction because the murder didn't happen on land, but they need help, and we work together."

"You're sure it's a murder?" Lou asked. "How about electrocution, suicide, heart attack…"

"Trust me, Lou. I know murder when I see it. This is murder."

"Ok, I'll be there," Lou promised. "Let your officers know I'm coming. I don't need hassles."

"For you, Lou, an escort," Chief McFadden replied. "A squad car should pull up to the Book Mark in about a minute. Thanks."

"Sure."

"Please sign my book, before you go, Lou," Doris said, afraid she would miss her reason for getting to the book store in advance of the signing.

"Oh, sure." Lou signed the book, "To Doris, Here we go again, literally. Guess the next book will probably begin with you. Enjoy *Poaching Man and Beast.* My best, Lou Searing."

Pat was left to explain to those in the ever-growing line that Lou had to leave; the rumors may be true, and a murder quite probably had occurred down by the pier. She promised an autographed copy for everyone in line, and she would make sure that Lou came back for handshakes, hugs, and reunions with fans. "Duty calls, folks," Pat said. "Guess you all are witnessing the beginning of the next Lou Searing mystery."

There were some moans and groans, but people knew that where there is a crime to be solved, Lou would want to be in the thick of things.

Standing in line for an autograph was Jack Kelly, a loyal fan. Jack, age 42, was blessed with a full head of hair and a goatee. He had a rounded face, a small nose, and a stocky build. When Lou left the Book Mark to get into the police car, Jack followed and also got in the vehicle. Lou thought nothing of it, believing he was one of the Chief's officers. The officer driving the squad car thought Lou was bringing an assistant.

"What's going on?" Lou asked the officer, now moving west on River Street at Code 2, choosing not to have the siren on.

"A fisherman spotted a foot hanging over the edge of the catwalk quite close to the light. Body was face up."

"Man or woman?" Jack asked. Lou glanced at Jack thinking he was one of Mickey's undercover officers.

"Woman," the officer replied.

"Do you know who she is?" Lou asked.

"No, middle-aged lady."

"How was she killed?" Lou asked.

"Haven't a clue at this point — the body is still on the catwalk. Last I heard — we're waiting for the medical examiner. Summer is always a difficult time to get the medical examiner, with golfing and vacations and all."

"Yeah, but with cell phones, seems like the ME is a phone call away."

"If he chooses to answer it."

"So, has Mickey seen the body?" Lou asked.

"Yeah, he and the Coast Guard have been up on the catwalk. They have the pier cordoned off. It didn't make folks too happy — perch are biting this morning."

"No sense having EMTs take the body to the hospital?" Lou asked.

"Deader than a door nail or at least that's what the chief says."

Lou Searing liked lighthouses, but he wasn't enough of a fan to go on tours or collect books. He did, however, enjoy seeing them on his travels around the state.

As a boy growing up in Grand Haven, he recalled many summer days perch fishing off the Grand Haven Pier, at whose end was the lighthouse. He had never walked the catwalk to the light and therefore had never gone inside. In fact, there were signs prohibiting unauthorized people from being up on the catwalk.

The squad car arrived at the pier. Lou and Jack, with notepad in hand, exited the car and pushed through the crowd that had gathered to watch. Lou walked up to Chief McFadden and shook hands with Manistee's highly-respected law enforcement leader. Mickey was stocky, strong, and good-looking. He reminded citizens of Matt Dillon of Gunsmoke. People knew Mickey meant business. The law was to be followed, and it generally was.

"Who is this? Maggie's replacement?" Mickey asked, nodding toward Jack, remembering that Maggie McMillan had helped Lou with a number of earlier cases.

"No, he just jumped in the squad car back at the Book Mark. He's one of your men, isn't he?" Lou replied.

"Mr. Searing, my name is Jack Kelly. I'm a big fan of yours. I took a chance and got in the car with you. I figured you could use some help."

"Rather bold move, Jack. I don't think I need any help. I don't want to make a scene here. Just stick with me and we'll straighten this out later."

"Thank you, sir," Jack said respectfully.

"Yes, he's with me, Chief. His name is Jack. Jack, this is Chief McFadden, one of the best in the business."

Chief McFadden shook Jack's hand. "Thanks for coming right out — probably left some unhappy people back at the Book Mark."

"I guess so. I see the medical examiner is here," Lou said as he watched someone inspecting the body up on the catwalk.

"Yeah, he got here a couple of minutes ago. Once he finishes, we'll get the body down and the Coast Guard will take it to the county morgue. I don't want to take the body bag through that summer beach crowd — too many kids. So, the Guardsmen will take the body in their launch to the station across the channel, and then an ambulance will take her to the hospital."

"Your officer didn't have much information for me on the way out here."

"We don't know much, Lou."

"Excuse me," Jack said. "Lou told me to stay out of the way, but, if I could ask, was there a crossword puzzle on the body?"

"As a matter of fact there was," Chief McFadden replied, quite taken aback that someone would know that.

"Lou, is this guy a suspect?" Chief McFadden said, pointing at Jack.

Lou was also dumbfounded by the question. "Yeah, what kind of a question is that?"

"Well, the keeper who was murdered at the light on Squaw Island in 1925 had a crossword puzzle on his chest when he was found."

"Excuse me?" Lou replied.

"Those of us who are into lighthouse lore know quite a bit about their history."

"Maybe you will be good for something, Jack," Lou said, patting Jack on the shoulder. Jack smiled, knowing that with that little piece of information, he might have earned his right to be on the team, so to speak.

"To answer your question, there was a small book of crossword puzzles next to her body," Chief McFadden replied looking at Jack. "I put it in an evidence bag. We'll dust it for prints and make sure the lab guys give it a good going over."

"Anything odd about it?" Lou asked.

Before Chief McFadden could answer, Jack said, "It's a full puzzle, except for one incomplete word."

"Is this guy some kind of psychic, Lou?" the chief asked with a smile.

"News to me," Lou replied, with a shrug of his shoulders.

"Yeah, that's right, Jack," McFadden said. "There was an incomplete puzzle. I didn't notice if a word was incomplete. We'll find out, though."

"Thanks, that should be helpful," said Jack, nodding his head.

The body had been lowered to the pier. Lou looked closely at it. From some gray hair the woman appeared to be in her early forties. She had been wearing a cap with an insignia of a lighthouse and the words, HOMES Lighthouse Tours. She was wearing sneakers, light blue slacks and a white sleeveless blouse. Her skin was pale, but he saw no blood, no wounds. She looked like she had lain down for a rest. The only problem was that she wasn't breathing.

Lou's cell phone rang. "Excuse me, men. Hello."

"Lou, this is Carol. Where are you?"

"Right now I am at the end of the pier in Manistee."

"Signing books? Honestly, you…"

"No, I left the signing because there's been a murder out on the pier, and Chief McFadden wanted my help."

"I see. Well, Stan Fedewa called. He wants you to help with a Knights of Columbus dinner tomorrow night, and I didn't know your schedule. He'd like to know if he could count on you."

"I don't know where this investigation will take me. I'll help if I can, but I can't commit. Sorry."

"Ok, I'll call him. We were going with the Beekmans to a movie tonight, remember? I assume that's history"

"I'm not sure. If there is nothing I can do here, I'll come home, but if I get involved in this thing, this has the higher priority. You go; I can't hear most of the movie anyway. You'll have company and can fill me in when I get home."

"OK. Be careful."

"I will. Don't worry. I'll call later. Love you." Lou put his phone in his pocket.

"So, Carol knows you are into another mystery, huh, Lou?" Jack said, knowing from reading his books that she is not keen on Lou's taking on dangerous criminals.

"Yup, she's cool with it. She worries, but she knows it's what I do and what I enjoy, so she's resigned to that. I promised to be careful and I meant it."

The medical examiner walked over to Chief McFadden while Lou and Jack moved closer to listen. "She's all yours, Chief. I'll get going on the report. Right now, I have no idea about the cause of death; the autopsy will give us a clue about that. There is some bruising, but no wounds that would cause death, no evidence of a fall; I don't smell anything that would indicate a poisoning. Sorry I'm not much help. Maybe your staff will find something, but I'm blank at this point. She could have been here last night. It's hard to tell. Rigor mortis is evident, so she didn't die in the last few hours; I'm certain of that."

"Ok, thanks, Doc," Chief McFadden said. "We'll get her to the morgue and keep investigating."

The doctor looked at Lou, nodded, and said, "Good afternoon, Mr. Searing." Lou returned the nod.

When the doc had left, Lou asked Mickey, "How did he know who I was?"

"The marina murders, Lou. In Manistee you could be the Grand Marshal for the Victorian Parade. You're pretty popular in these parts."

"That's hard to believe. I investigated one murder — that's all it takes to become grand marshal of a parade?"

"It was the way you did it, Lou. You were nice to that little kid who discovered the body. You were kind to Rose Crandall, the senior citizen who kept an eye on the harbor from her apartment.

You were respectful of my staff and the people at the hospital. People remember good people, Lou."

"Yeah, but Grand Marshal in the Victorian Parade?"

"Ok, maybe I exaggerated a bit there. They like you in Manistee. I'll leave it at that."

"They like him wherever he has been," Jack said. "Lou is sort of like the Lone Ranger. He isn't forgotten. He doesn't leave a silver bullet; he just leaves the murder solved and justice in its place."

As the body was being lowered into the launch, Lou and Jack began a serious look around the light. They didn't find any obvious clues. The structure was simply a frame for the light. The actual light was now automatic and was visited by the Coast Guard for occasional cleaning and inspection.

"You got a theory on this murder?" Lou asked Jack.

"Oh no, that's your job," Jack replied. I'm just here to help you. Like Sancho in *Man of La Mancha,* I shine your boots, polish your sword, and tend to your horse. You go after the windmills."

"My shoes are kind of scruffy," Lou mused, looking down at his loafers.

"You know what I mean. I'm not a servant in the true sense of the word, but you know what I'm talking about. I just want to help."

"Just pulling your leg, Jack. By the way, in that murder at the Squaw Island Light, how did the victim die?"

"A ghost turned on the stove's gas jets."

"No way," Lou replied.

"Just checking whether you can separate fact from the ridiculous, Lou."

"I've heard a lot of stories, but ghosts turning on gas jets has not been one of them. Ghosts might open a door, or turn a light on and off, but planning and executing a murder — I don't think so."

"I agree."

"I suppose the ghost left the crossword puzzle on the body, too?" Lou asked sarcastically.

"I can't answer that."

The police concluded their investigation of the area around noon. Photos had been taken; any suspicious items were picked up and identified. Portions of the light were dusted for prints and inspected thoroughly. One of the officers proposed that the woman simply climbed up to the catwalk where she wasn't supposed to be and had a heart attack. Jack quickly interjected after hearing the theory, "And the crossword puzzle on her body?"

"Oh yeah, forgot about that," the officer replied. "That is a bit strange. Never mind."

Lou asked a Coast Guardsman, "Do you folks have any kind of surveillance in the channel?"

"Video recording — is that what you mean?"

"I suppose so. You know, like they have in stores and parking lots."

"No, we don't."

"You should," Lou advised. "I think you should think about it. In this day of fear and terrorism, it seems like you'd want to monitor who comes and goes into this channel."

"I hear you, but you're talking to the wrong guy. You got an issue with our procedures, you need the Commanding Officer, not a nobody like me."

"Chief," Lou shouted, trying to get Mickey's attention as he stood several feet from the light.

"Yeah, Lou?"

Lou moved closer to Mickey. "I need you to tell me what calls, if any, you get from people who may have seen or heard something suspicious."

"No problem. I'll let you know."

"Thanks. I'm going to leave now, Chief. We'll be in touch."

Lou and Jack went back to the Book Mark where Lou apologized to Pat for his quick exit and for disappointing people. Pat understood. "It was lucky for Chief McFadden though. He respects your work, Lou. Your being here has probably cut several days off the time it will take to solve it."

"I don't know about that, but we'll do the best we can."

"I have a list of people who want your autograph," Pat replied. "So, if you could sign copies before you leave, I'll call the customers tomorrow, and they can pick up their books."

Lou called Carol to say that he would not be home for dinner and the movie. Once the books were signed, Lou and Jack went to The House That Jack Built for something to eat and some planning before they headed south to Grand Haven and Muskegon, respectively.

The first thing Lou noticed at the restaurant was the attention given to his new assistant. *This man must be one loyal customer who hands out pretty good tips to be treated with such respect,* Lou thought. Most knew Jack by name, smiled, and made sure he was comfortable and served well.

"Thanks for letting me tag along, Lou," Jack said sincerely.

"Sure. When you jumped in the squad car at the Book Mark, for all I knew you were one of Chief McFadden's undercover men."

"No, just a huge fan of yours, but I saw an opportunity to learn something, so I took a chance. You've got to take chances in life, Lou, or an entire lifetime goes by like a bullet fired from a gun. If you had shoved me into the channel, it would have been no big deal. I'd still have a story — pushed off the Manistee pier by the famous detective, Lou Searing."

"You really were impressive when you knew about that murder at the lighthouse," Lou said. "Where was that again?"

"Squaw Island. It's in Lake Michigan, northwest of Beaver Island; part of that group of off-shore islands between Escanaba and Charlevoix."

"Tell me about that murder," Lou asked over a hot cup of vegetable beef soup and a slice of garlic bread.

"Well, the story goes that the keeper and his family lived in the light where he was killed."

"How did the keeper die?" Lou asked.

"Don't know."

"Why was he murdered?"

"I don't know."

"Who killed the keeper?" Lou continued his questions.

"Don't know. I don't think it was ever solved."

"Out on the pier with the police and Coast Guard you were a fountain of information. Now, you're dry as a bone," Lou said, shaking his head.

"Sorry, but there was a murder at the Squaw Island Light, and there was a crossword puzzle left on the body."

"You sure, Jack? You're not pulling my leg?" Lou asked. "We hard-of-hearing people are pretty gullible."

"It's not just me talking," Jack said, frustrated not to be taken seriously. "This is in every lighthouse book written."

"So, today we have a murder outside another light, and a crossword puzzle is left on the body. I mean, tell me the chances of that happening twice about 85 years apart," Lou asked.

"Pretty low, I would imagine."

"When did this murder happen on Squaw Island?" Lou asked.

"1925."

"So, this sure isn't a copy-cat murder."

"Not unless someone really knew lighthouse history and wanted to replay the drama," Jack replied.

"Not likely."

"I agree."

"I'm curious about this crossword puzzle," Lou said. "Does a copy of it exist?"

"I don't know," Jack replied.

"Well, we've got something to go on."

"I like your pronoun, Lou," Jack said. "Can I help you with this one? I think I'll be worth your time. I'd appreciate it if you'd give me a shot. I have many skills and some of them might come in handy."

"For example?"

"I'm a pretty good lip reader, believe it or not," Jack said, not believing that Lou was impressed. "Please give me a trial run, okay?"

"I guess that'd be all right. I don't have a reason to say no, and you've already earned your dinner. We'll continue to work together, and if it rolls along, fine. If not, it will be obvious that one of us needs to call it off."

"You'll not regret this, Lou. This is the best thing that's ever happened to me!"

"Oh, I doubt that," Lou said, shaking his head. "Since we're going to be working on this, tell me a little about yourself."

"I went to Muskegon Schools and finished my formal education with a master's degree in Business Management at Aquinas College in Grand Rapids."

"No Ph.D. in Contemporary Literature or anything like that?" Lou asked.

"Actually, now you must be psychic. I am an ABD — all but the dissertation — in Religions of the World, but like a lot of students, life came at me from all sides. And, well, I just never got around to finishing the dissertation."

"The title of which was?" Lou asked.

"The Concept of Sin and Redemption, as Portrayed in Major Religions."

"That's got to cry out for some excitement," Lou said, sarcastically. "Sorry to make fun of your passion."

"I don't blame you. It's not the most exciting topic, and maybe that's why I never finished the thing."

"How did life come at you from all sides?" Lou asked, using the question to get to know Jack a little better.

"Relationships, career, illness," Jack responded. "You know, just living life. Somehow the dissertation slipped to the back burner, and I just never got back to it."

"It happens. Life, I mean."

"Yeah, I know," Jack said, picking up his coffee cup.

The waitress came by, "Good afternoon, Mr. Kelly."

"Hi, Shelly. Shelly, this is the famous detective, Lou Searing."

"Nice to meet you, Mr. Searing." Lou nodded and smiled. "We'll have to take your picture with Mr. Kelly and hang it on our wall of celebrities."

"Sure, we'll do that when we finish," Jack added.

"Wall of celebrities?" Lou asked, confused.

"There is a wall on the other side of the restaurant with photos of celebrities who have visited the restaurant," Shelly said.

"But you said to take the picture with Mr. Kelly."

"Well, yes, I'm in most of the photos," Jack replied.

"Who are some of the celebrities?" Lou asked.

"Well, for starters there are sports personalities — I like sports. There are photos of Al Kaline, Joe Louis, Bobby Layne, Rocky Marciano, Jack Nicklaus, Tiger Woods…"

"They've all been here?" Lou asked, awed.

"Not all of them. Most of those photos were taken somewhere else."

"What famous people have actually been here?" Lou asked.

"You mean in addition to you?"

"Don't be ridiculous."

"Let's see. Actually been here? Now we need to move into the world of entertainers. So, that would include Tom Cruise, Russell Crowe, and Gwyenth Paltrow… "

"Really? Here in Manistee?"

"Hey, Lou, these are just people. They travel, visit friends. They don't just sit in Hollywood, or wherever."

"Well, I know, but why come here to this restaurant?"

"To see me."

"You?"

"There's quite a story behind this restaurant, Lou."

Suddenly, it hit Lou. "The House That Jack Built. You're Jack."

"I'm Jack."

"Really? Interesting. So this is your job?" Lou asked.

"No. I pay people to run this. This is my escape, my space in the world where dreams come true."

"What is your real job then?"

"I'm finance director for Gospel Communications in Muskegon."

"Quite a calling."

"I think so. Bringing Jesus Christ to people is my passion, and I handle the finances for the company. Doesn't sound like much, and it isn't, but it's my way of giving back."

"Giving back?"

"Another story, for another time."

"I'll look forward to hearing it."

"We'll get along just fine," Jack concluded. "I need to be sure you get what you need, whether it's information, clues, advice, or probably most of the time, just getting out of the way."

"Two rules, Jack." Lou was once again serious.

"I bet I can guess. Speak when spoken to, and be accurate. Am I right?" Jack asked.

"Those are a couple of good ones, but no. My rules are first, don't embarrass me, and second, give me no surprises."

"That's it, only two?"

"Only two, but they're big ones," Lou emphasized. "Anyone who knows me well knows I don't like to be surprised, and I don't like to look bad."

"No one does," Jack replied.

"Especially me. I'll give anyone credit — I don't need that — but please, no surprises, and no embarrassment."

"Well, I've got one rule, and I feel as strongly as you feel about your two."

"What's that?"

"Don't lie to me," Jack said stoically. "All it takes is one lie. I'll forgive, but I won't forget. One lie and it takes a long time to restore the trust."

"That might be a problem with some suspects we run into, but you're working with a man who has the same values."

Lou got the attention of the waitress. "Check, please. One bill, and give it to me."

"Won't take your money, Lou. This is on the house," Jack said.

Two cars left the restaurant heading south, Lou to Grand Haven and Jack to Muskegon. While paying attention to the road and listening to a CD, Lou kept thinking about this dead woman on the catwalk by the light. Who was she? How did she get up there unnoticed? And why was she dead? Answers were sure to come in time. The case would be challenging.

Jack drove in a state of disbelief. He had gone to Manistee to get an autographed copy of Lou's book, and now he was an assistant to a well-thought-of detective and already significantly involved in a crime. It was almost too much to comprehend. "Am I in heaven or what?" Jack shouted to the cows in a field north of the New Era exit on Highway 31.

That night on the 6 o'clock television news, viewers heard.

The lead story this evening is Murder at the Manistee Lighthouse.

Police say a fisherman reported seeing a foot protruding from the catwalk above the pier near the Manistee Light this morning. The victim is a middle-aged woman who is not yet identified. Police are asking that anyone who saw the woman on the catwalk or noticed anything suspicious in the area of the Manistee Light to please call the number on your screen. You don't need to leave your name. There is no indication of how the woman died and if she was murdered, there are no suspects at this hour. The body has been transported to the County Hospital, where an autopsy is planned for tomorrow.

The police and Coast Guard have cordoned off the area, expecting to allow citizens back on the pier tomorrow. Police Chief Mickey McFadden believes the town is safe and he sees no reason for citizens to be concerned for their safety. More at eleven.

On July 7, an autopsy on the woman who had died on the cat-walk in Manistee determined the cause of death to be poisoning. There were also bruises on the body, indicating a struggle.

Chief McFadden got a call from Jack Cady, the chief of police in Rogers City. Apparently a neighbor of a woman named Frieda Bowman had contacted police when Frieda failed to return from a lighthouse tour on the Wisconsin side of Lake Michigan.

"The neighbor told me she cares for Miss Bowman's cat," Chief Cady said. "Miss Bowman lives alone, has no family, and just comes and goes, especially in the summer, doing a lot of lighthouse tours."

"Can you get me some prints, or maybe something for DNA?" Mickey asked.

"I'll fax a photo right now. That'll help you with a preliminary ID."

"Thanks. And, no next of kin that you know of?"

"That's right."

The faxed photo arrived shortly and the dead woman on the catwalk appeared to be Miss Bowman. If it wasn't the same woman, they were twin sisters.

Shortly after the body was identified and the name made available to the media, Chief McFadden received a call from the manager of the *Dam In The River Casino*.

"I'm not saying there is a connection, Chief, but that woman on the catwalk in Manistee is one of our best customers. She was a compulsive gambler and dealt in big bucks with unsavory characters. Just letting you know."

"I appreciate the call. It gives us a place to start."

The biggest clue in the Bowman murder investigation was the crossword puzzle book found near Frieda's body. CSI analysis produced no leads. There were no fingerprints, nothing unique about the letters, or how they were formed. The killer probably wanted to play a game, a brain-game, to see if the police would be confused, challenged, or able to match wits with him, her, or them.

Lou was into crossword puzzles, those books that advertised them as "EASY." He could do those in the local newspaper to about seventy-five percent completion, and then Carol would need to polish them off or give him some answers that opened the door to getting a few more across or down. Solving a *New York Times* puzzle was totally out of the question.

But it was important to Lou and Jack to know what was written in the puzzle that was in Frieda's pocket when she died. Lou asked Mickey to give him the information. A phone call was all it took. The answer was that the puzzle was complete except for one word. The clue was 'not at any time' and the letters that were written into the spaces were E and R with the first three spaces left blank.

Lou was willing to match wits with the killer. In fact, the chase and capture was more like a chess match than a game of vocabulary prowess. However it was viewed, it was Lou looking for a killer, and if past were prologue, Lou would win. It was just a matter of time.

$$\boxed{7}$$

The day was July 9 and the Kammeraad Funeral Home in Reed City was about to move to a state-of-the-art facility across town. The decision to contract with a reputable moving company had been made and it was time to make arrangements.

"Two Men and a Truck, how may I direct your call?"

"This is J.W. at the Kammeraad Funeral Home. I'd like to arrange a move."

"One moment please."

After a few seconds J.W. heard, "This is Wayne Conn. How can we be of service to you?"

"I would like to contract with you to move the contents of a funeral home, and I don't plan to solicit bids. Your company is top-notch as far as I am concerned, so I just need to get a quote and agree on a date."

"Thank you for the compliment," Wayne replied. "This could be a first for us. I don't think we've ever moved a funeral home before."

"I agree it's not common, but we've built a state-of-the-art facility outside of town and we need professional movers to be responsible for getting us from here to there, if you know what I mean."

"Yes, and moving is our business, so we'll do a great job for you," Mr. Conn assured Mr. Kammeraad. "Can you give me some idea of the items to be moved?"

"We have two offices, four viewing rooms. Downstairs we have the caskets on display and the equipment in the room for burial preparation."

"So, we will have several chairs, living room furniture, office furniture, caskets, and laboratory equipment. Did I hear you correctly?" Wayne asked.

"Basically, yes. There will be a few bodies in transition, but that will be no problem," J.W. added.

"A few bodies? Dead bodies?" Wayne asked apprehensively.

"Yes. What other kind of bodies would we have in a funeral home?" Mr. Kammeraad asked with a chuckle.

"Comes with the territory, I guess. These bodies, are they in caskets or …"

"No, they will not be in caskets but in bags."

"I see. Okay. Let's see when this move can take place. Would Monday, the 12th be okay?" Wayne asked.

"Yes, actually that would be perfect. We will close on that day so the place will be yours to empty. Our Open House will be one week later and that will give us time to unpack and be ready for guests."

"Guests don't really care what the place looks like, right?" Wayne asked, with a hint of humor in his voice.

"Excuse me?" J.W. asked.

"Sorry, I was thinking the guests were the dead people."

"No, these guests will be dignitaries, business leaders, and those who have pre-arranged their funerals with us."

"Well, whoever they are, they will appreciate your new home, I am sure. It is your decision but I would recommend four men and two trucks so everything can be moved in about a half-day."

"Fine. I am not as concerned about cost as I am about the professionalism of your workers. I don't want a scratch. Our furniture is the best, and I want it delivered perfectly."

"That won't be a problem, Mr. Kammeraad."

"Excellent. Thank you."

"We'll send you the agreement, including our fee, and an offer to purchase boxes if you need them. We'll work with you to see that you are totally satisfied."

As soon as the handset hit the cradle, Mr. Conn called his moving supervisor, Charles James, for truck assignments.

"Charlie, we've got a strange job coming up. I need to clue you in on what is going to happen. I want the right men assigned. There must be absolutely no mistakes on this job."

"Not a problem. What's the move?"

"We've been contracted to relocate the Kammeraad Funeral Home in Reed City."

"Piece of cake — chairs, furniture, a few caskets."

"And a few dead people," Wayne added.

"Tell them to call a cab — we're only into non-living stuff."

"This is non-living stuff, Charlie. They expect to have about four corpses. That's what they usually have, and business has been good lately."

"Nah, they'll put them in caskets and take them over in hearses," Charlie suggested. "They don't want us fooling with their customers; well, you know what I mean."

"I agree, but they want us to move everything, and that includes bodies waiting for services."

"At least the dead won't be giving us any lip," Charlie said. "I hate it when our customers try to get in our way of doing the job."

"They'll be out of the way and silent," Wayne replied. "You can bet on that. Listen Charlie; make sure the inventory is accurate, I want every chair counted, every piece of furniture, and yes, every body counted as it goes into trucks. I know that place, and the cost to us to replace a chair or sofa — don't want to talk about it. Buying just one piece of furniture could wipe out our profit margin."

"I'll take care of the inventory," Charlie promised. "You just assign guys that are mature enough to handle this job — dead furniture and dead people. You don't need anything dropped, and especially not someone's beloved aunt. I'll handle it, Mr. Conn."

"That's why I assigned you to the move, Charlie. You make us look good and for this job, we need to look good, very good."

The relocation of the Kammeraad Funeral Home was a major event. The Kammeraad Funeral Home had been in downtown Reed City for many years and the Kammeraads were well into their third and fourth generation of burials for the town's most distinguished citizens as well as the paupers from the county jail and a few homeless folks with no families.

The move to the new facility outside of town was worthy of a newspaper article. On July 11, it appeared on the front page of the *Reed City News:*

Kammeraad Funeral Home to Relocate

The Kammeraad Funeral Home is proud to announce that the community is invited to an Open House at their new facility, 1100 Worthington Blvd. on Monday, July 19. According to President J.W. Kammeraad, this new facility will be the most modern and beautiful funeral home in all of North America. It has every convenience one can imagine to meet the needs of a grieving family. Two Men and a Truck have contracted to move the funeral home to its new location. Mr. J.W. Kammeraad, CEO, announced that the family of the first person buried from the new funeral home will receive a free casket and floral spray.

8

JULY 10

One week following the murder of Frieda Bowman as Lou and Samm, the Searing's golden retriever, were traveling to a meeting with Tom and Fran Howard to help plan the annual Coast Guard Festival in Grand Haven, Lou's cell phone rang. The phone display indicated that Carol was calling. He pulled to the side of the road, reached for a pencil and notepad, and answered the phone.

"Lou, Linda Clymer just called from Ludington. A man was found dead at the Big Sable Point Lighthouse. Her neighbor is the manager there, and Linda wanted you to know because she's aware that you're helping Chief McFadden with the murder in Manistee."

"OK. Who am I to call? Did she say?" Lou asked.

"Mickey McFadden. And, Lou, there's one more thing. There was a crossword puzzle on top of the body."

"Thanks, I'll call Mickey."

"Be careful, Lou. Let me know if you head to Ludington. I love you."

"I will. Love you, too."

Lou then called Mickey. "The murder is not within my jurisdiction, Lou. I got a call from the Mason County sheriff because he knew about my case from reading a bulletin."

"What do you know so far?" Lou asked.

"Well, that crossword puzzle business is consistent with what we found on the catwalk. But this guy's been identified: his name is Arthur Webberson, an older gentleman, from the Detroit area, a big fan of lighthouses, and a man with money and influence."

"He has nothing but a metal slab in the mortuary now, but I hope he enjoyed it while he had it," Lou said. "That could have been his downfall."

"That's often the case."

"Jack and I will go to Ludington," Lou replied. "Can you let the Mason County sheriff know we'll be there in about an hour or so?"

"I'll handle it," Chief McFadden promised. "Looks like these two are related, Lou."

"It does seem possible. I'll get right on this, Chief."

Lou called Jack and asked him to meet him at the Big Sable Light north of the Ludington State Park.

Lou arrived at Big Sable Point about noon, two hours after talking with Mickey. A sheriff's deputy, Candice Vogel met Lou at the gate. The two vehicles moved down the quarter-mile sandy road to the lighthouse. There was another police vehicle in the parking area when they arrived. The sheriff wanted to be at the light when Lou arrived. Lou was surprised to see that Jack was already on-site, taking notes and asking questions.

Once inside, and after some discussion about the role Lou and Jack would play in the investigation, Lou and Jack got right to work. "I'll need a list of everyone who was here when the murder occurred," Lou said. "Actually, make that for several days before the murder."

"Got it, Lou," Deputy Vogel replied.

"Good. Have you interviewed any of them?"

"Only the volunteers on duty at the time of the alleged murder."

"Did you get any helpful information?" Lou asked.

"Not really."

"Were tourists in the area?" Jack asked.

"There were several dignitaries from town and several media types. Webberson was going to hold a press conference and never showed up."

The television news report was emphatic,

Self-made millionaire and long-time lighthouse association benefactor Arthur Webberson was reportedly found dead at the Big Sable Point Lighthouse north of Ludington. A crossword puzzle was found with the body when police learned of Mr. Webberson's death at mid-morning Friday. At this time, police have no witnesses and no motive for the slaying. More during our evening newscast.

Arthur Webberson's intention to visit the Big Sable Point Lighthouse was no secret. His itinerary was usually known to at least a dozen people, including his secretary and his wife. The chairman of the HOMES Lighthouse Association was always informed when Arthur would visit a lighthouse, and it would be very easy for the HOMES Board, family members or even the general public to know Arthur Webberson's schedule.

Arthur had traveled to Ludington to conduct a press conference to kick off National Lighthouse Month. He would expound on the beauty of Michigan lighthouses, announce a number of tours and events, and read a proclamation from the Governor. He was planning to have a little fun as well, encouraging people to come to the Big Sable Lighthouse in hopes of meeting its friendly ghost, Henry. Stories about Henry were numerous, but Henry's activities were probably figments of the imaginations of people wanting Henry to appear. With that idea in place, it doesn't take much for people to "see" or "hear" something, or notice a door ajar or something that had fallen to the floor.

The press conference was well-orchestrated. A few HOMES Lighthouse Association Board members were present, as were several members of the media. Even the local television station was on hand.

Through a cold and drizzly Michigan summer morning, a train of umbrellas made their way from the parking lot to the light. The fog, with an occasional breeze, seemed to give people an eerie feeling that reminded them of Jolly Old England or the Scottish moors. Thankfully, the drizzle yielded to sun as the press conference was about to begin.

Reporters and important people gathered outside the lighthouse where microphones were set up at a small podium. At ten a.m., June Liberty, the chair of the Ludington Chapter of the HOMES Lighthouse Association thanked those present for coming to the press conference, mentioned that coffee and some light refreshments were available on a table to her left, and informed them that Mr. Webberson was upstairs in the keeper's home and would be joining them momentarily.

When Arthur didn't appear, June went up to let him know that the visitors were waiting. She knocked and there was no response. She knocked again, then slowly opened the door, asking, "Mr. Webberson, are you there? Mr. Webberson?" The room appeared undisturbed except for a handwritten note on a table near the door. She picked it up and read, *"Mr. Webberson has died and has been taken to a funeral home. Apologize to your guests and suggest they leave."*

Mrs. Liberty, feeling light-headed, quickly sank into a chair. Nothing was out of place, but Arthur's speech lay on the bed. There was no other trace of him.

June collected herself and tried not to panic, but decided to apologize to all present, explain that the press conference was cancelled, and encourage people to pick up materials and take what refreshments were left. HOMES Board members were curious why this important media event was cancelled. June simply said, "Mr. Webberson is not here and the entire presentation was his message."

Once the place was vacated, June called the sheriff to report what she had experienced.

What surprised Lou and Jack at the Big Sable Point Light was the absence of a body to view and that the medical examiner had not stopped by. There was only the note saying Webberson had died. Deputy Vogel had heard a rumor that the victim was found at the base of the Light, and that he had an unfinished crossword puzzle on his body. Whoever found him apparently had taken him to a funeral home.

"That can't be," Lou said to Jack.

"Not in this day and age," Jack replied.

"Who took his body?" Lou asked Miss Vogel.

"We don't know. We got a call from a funeral home saying the body was there."

"The funeral home didn't require the body be turned over to the medical examiner?" Lou asked, stunned with what he was hearing.

"Guess not."

"How can we even be sure this guy died?" Jack asked.

"We can't," said Deputy Vogel. "We're here looking for evidence of a crime, and Chief McFadden suggested to the sheriff that you become involved."

"What's the name of the funeral home?" Lou asked.

"They didn't say."

"Your phone log has the call in its data base, right?" Jack asked.

"No, whoever called from the funeral home used a cell phone."

"From a funeral home?" Jack replied. "This isn't adding up."

"Someone's playing games," Lou reasoned.

"Big-time," Jack replied. "What can you tell us about the crossword puzzle?"

"Whoever called from the funeral home said the puzzle was complete except for one word, where all the letters were filled in except one. The clue was 'predict low' and the letters in place were all but the last one; U.N.D.E.R.E.S.T.I.M.A.T.__. The missing letter was obviously an E.

Lou turned to Miss Vogel and asked, "I assume you have an all-points bulletin out for law enforcement offices to contact local funeral homes in hopes of finding the body?"

"Yes, the sheriff has already done that, and we've checked with Ludington funeral homes, and the body is not there."

"Guess we'll be on our way. You or the sheriff will let Chief McFadden know of any developments, correct?"

"Yes, I'm sure our offices will be working on these crimes together. We may have a copy-cat crime here."

"Or a murder and a neat plan of deceit," Lou replied.

As Lou and Jack headed for their vehicles, Lou said, "Sorry to ask you to come up here for nothing, Jack."

"Hey, no problem. Some bits of information are duds and some blaze like fireworks. At least we know about a second murder."

"I'm not convinced of a second murder," Lou said. "I mean, no body, no formal procedures. I've seen high school pranks that were more convincing. I bet if we called this Webberson guy, he'd answer the phone."

"Might be worth a call," Jack said.

Lou said to Jack, "Listen, I'll stay here in Ludington and work on these two cases. I assume you'll head home to Muskegon?"

"Yes. I'm only an hour away if you need me, and phone and e-mail should be sufficient. Want to have a sandwich before I go?"

"Good idea," Lou replied. "Let me buy this time."

9

JULY 11

In a B and B in Ludington, Michigan, Lou turned on his laptop and entered "lighthouse murders" into the subject bar. A few seconds later a few items were visible. He chose the one titled, "Tragedy at Squaw Island Lighthouse," opened the item, and read a fascinating report. His eyes quickly scanned the essay until he came to the middle of the page, where Lou started reading each word carefully.

> The man who investigated the murder said that he could find no motive, no weapon, nor any clue that would lead him to the murderer, save one interesting observation. After the son admitted the murder in 1961, the bones of the victim were exhumed and resting on the bones was an unfinished crossword puzzle. The letters that were written following an empty first space were R.E.E.D., and the clue for seven down was 'having an overwhelming desire for something.'

Lou instantly knew that the word was "Greed" and wondered what would cause someone to stop half-way through a word, much less to place the uncompleted puzzle in the grave.

Lou called Carol on his cell phone. The two of them talked to each other every day, keeping a promise they made after their wedding.

"Just checking in," Lou began.

"I'm glad you did. There was a message on the answering machine when I got home from church."

"I'm all ears."

"You might want to get pencil and paper," Carol said. "It really didn't make any sense to me, so I repeated it a few times and took down exactly what the man said. Ready?"

"Yup. Go ahead."

"OK, the caller was a man, who said 'Mr. Searing. I have learned that you are investigating the lighthouse murders in west Michigan. I suggest you look at the *USA Today* puzzle for today, clue thirteen across. There are five letters in the word and the first four letters are P.O.W.E, and the clue is 'horse _____.' One more thing: ask yourself why Professor Wilkenson finds it necessary to begin his lecture telling the audience about a murder. You are a master at solving crime, Mr. Searing, but you have met your match. There is simply no way you can solve this one. I leave you with great respect for your abilities'."

"Got it?" Carol asked.

"Let me read it back to you," Lou said. He had written the message exactly as Carol had read it. "Did you keep an audio copy of this?" he asked.

"No, I made sure I got every word, but before I thought you would need to hear it, I let it get away from me. Sorry."

"A voice analysis might have been helpful down the line, but the message is the important part."

"What does he mean about a puzzle and some letters in the answer? Wasn't a crossword puzzle part of the last murder?" Carol asked.

"Yes. I need to make sense of it."

"You will," Carol replied. "Like everyone else, I'm always amazed at your uncanny ability to solve these things."

"It's just a lot of luck," Lou replied. "A lot like putting a puzzle together without having the picture on the box to match your patterns."

"Did you get something to eat?" Carol asked.

"Yes, Jack and I got a sandwich."

"Jack? Who's Jack?"

"Oh, I'll tell you about him when I get home. He is an interesting character who wants to help me."

"Where is he from?" Carol asked.

"Muskegon. He was at the book signing, and when one of Chief McFadden's officers picked me up, he just jumped in the car and joined the team, so to speak."

"Wasn't that a bit presumptuous?" Carol asked.

"Yeah, but stranger things have happened."

"Can he be trusted, Lou?"

"Far as I can tell. He's not just a tag-along; he's been quite a bit of help."

"Got a suspect yet in either murder?" Carol asked, always interested in Lou's work.

"Oh, no, I haven't any idea as to who the murderers are or why they murdered. That phone call is my first significant clue; the caller was probably the murderer. Well, sleep tight. By the way, you can always reach me on my cell, but I am at the Beach Side B and B in Ludington. Talk with you tomorrow. Love you."

"I miss you, Lou. Walking the beach is pretty lonely without you."

"I walked the beach late this afternoon and imagined you beside me all the way," Lou replied.

Although the caller had given him the crossword clue, Lou wanted a copy of the puzzle; there could be more information that might be helpful. Lou went to the 7-11 in town, but all copies of *USA Today* papers had been sold. He drove to a couple of convenience stores and found the same problem. Finally, he went to a drug store and asked the clerk if he had any *USA Today* newspapers for sale.

"Not for sale. I have one that I'm taking home, but I'll let you look at it. I'm not leaving here for a couple of hours. That should be enough time for you to read it."

"Thanks. Do you have a copy machine here?"

"It's over by the phone." Lou copied the puzzle, returned the newspaper, and left with what he hoped would be a helpful source of information.

When it came time for the Kammeraad Funeral Home move, Charlie decided this was a good day to train a fifth worker. There would be hundreds of folding chairs, and the new man could get his feet wet with the light and easy items. Plus, the company could boast to their client that they were actually getting five men and two trucks for the job.

The job went smoothly with furniture being wrapped in thick, padded covers and surrounded by plastic wrap to assure no damage. The office furniture was moved without incident. Finally, it was time to move the caskets and laboratory equipment. There were about twenty caskets on display and another fifty or so in crates. It took two men to move each casket on display plus those in the storeroom.

The heaviest items in the laboratory were the tanks of embalming fluid. This required special equipment which wasn't a problem, but it took time to prepare the items for moving.

Charlie also decided not to tell the workers about moving the dead bodies before the moving date. He called them over and said, "Listen guys. We're going to be moving some dead people who are in this next room."

"Wrong pronoun, boss," Garret Peterman said immediately. "'We're' is not the right word. I know I don't work for a union company, but this is not what I took this job to do."

"Think of it as a box, Garret. It is just a bunch of matter, like a stuffed sofa."

"Thanks, that helps a lot, boss," Kyle Eagen said sarcastically.

"Well, we've gotta move 'em, so do something else if this isn't something you can handle. The rest of us will move the bodies, right men?"

"Not a problem with me since you'll be giving us time-and-a-half for this part of the job, right boss?" Kyle asked, but meant it more as an ultimatum.

"If that's what it takes to get these stiffs to their new home, yeah, time-and-a-half. Now let's get 'em in the truck."

As each body was removed from the cooler and taken up to the truck, the company moving manager marked the name on the inventory sheet. Each body was secured into a crate-like structure that was solid and clean.

When the truck arrived at the new home, the first items off were the bodies. The reverse of all the work in the morning was ready to commence. The moving manager checked off each body that came off the truck. "Ok, we put four bodies on and we are delivering four bodies."

It was time for Lou to check in with the sheriff.

"How are you doing, 'Deputy'?" the sheriff asked.

"I'm basically working and talking to people. I haven't had any 'Aha' moments yet. I'm learning a lot, but each time I think I'm heading in the right direction, the mind takes a turn and I'm on a lonely road going nowhere. Has the obit appeared in a daily paper yet?"

"I am sure it was in the *Detroit Free Press*. A reporter called asking questions."

"I need to see the obit as soon as possible. Actually, never mind, I'll read it on the Internet." Lou checked, and in addition to the obit there was a three-column article honoring Webberson's philanthropy with several quotes from family, friends, and lighthouse admirers. Lou made a copy of the obit and the article. The short obituary read:

> *Arthur S. Webberson, age 65, of Bloomfield Hills, Michigan, passed away on July 10 in Ludington, Michigan. Mr. Webberson was one the metro area's finest philanthropists and a successful businessman making his fortune in components for the auto industry. He is survived by his wife, Florence, son, Wallace (Beatrice), and daughter, Victoria Wilkshire (Bertrand). He is also survived by a brother,*

Theodore. He was preceded in death by his parents, Sir Jonathan and Mrs.Webberson of London, England. Mr. Webberson had a passion for lighthouses around the world, but especially in Michigan and throughout England, Scotland, and Ireland. A memorial service will be held on Friday, July 17 at ten a.m. at the Big Sable Lighthouse, north of Ludington. In lieu of flowers, those wishing to offer a donation in Arthur's memory are encouraged to support the HOMES Lighthouse Association.

☐☐☐☐☐

One of a few people genuinely happy with the death announcement was Rose McCracken. She didn't know the man other than that he was a barrier to her obtaining her own lighthouse. She envisioned a tyrant, a greedy monster who stood boldly in the way of fulfilling her dreams. Rose was sitting at her computer searching for a rare, hard-to-find mystery written by Arthur Conan Doyle, when she decided to go to www.msnbc.com to see if there was any news of note. There it was, *"Arthur Webberson Murdered: Michigan Philanthropist Loved Lighthouses."* A smile came across her face as she realized that the fulfillment of finally owning a light could soon be real.

Mary came into the den within a few minutes of Rose's reading of the death. "Mary dear, guess what, guess what happened."

"The lighthouse man is dead."

To say that Rose was shocked would be putting it mildly. There was no way that Mary would know of this event, absolutely no way whatsoever. "How did you know this, honey?"

Mary said nothing for a minute. She simply stood in the middle of the room with Rose staring at her, waiting for a response. Finally, Mary looked at Rose and said, "This is what you wanted."

"I don't wish anyone dead, Mary. He was in the way of our owning our own light, yes, but, how did you know? How could you know?"

"I know."

"You must have had a dream or maybe I gave you too much of your medication, or maybe the wrong medication. I'm becoming careless?"

"The crossword puzzle word is 'Underestimate'."

"What word? What are you talking about?"

"Underestimate."

"Oh, honey. We've got to get you to the doctor. You're becoming delusional. We're going to Emergency."

Rose was beside herself with Mary's unexplainable behavior. How was it possible for her to know that Arthur was dead and know the uncompleted word in the crossword puzzle? At the emergency room, Mary was seen by a registered nurse and then a physician. They could find nothing wrong with her vital signs. She answered every question appropriately. And, there was no sign of drug side-effects. They simply had no suggestions for what Rose considered odd or exceptional behavior. The doctor rattled off a list of possible scenarios, but Rose had already thought of them: dream, thought-transfer, chance, and pre-cognition. After Mary was cleared at the hospital, she and Rose returned home, saying nothing to each other on the way.

Rose wasted little time in communicating with those who held claim to vacant lighthouses. Some had not heard that Arthur Webberson had died. All Rose wanted to know were the necessary steps to purchase a light. With Arthur's death, the door opened wide. There were some other interested parties and often they were preservation associations, or a city council or two. A university was most interested in another light. But, Rose was in luck because the Government Accounting Office was now free to offer her a lighthouse near Saugatuck, Michigan. There was even a keeper's home for a bed and breakfast. Rose looked forward to creating a very warm and unique little inn.

"Perfect!" Rose shouted into the phone. "My dream has come true. My dream has come true!" Before the phone call was complete, arrangements had been made for a transfer of funds and deed. Rose was simply in the right place at the right time. She could acquire the light and move in within days. She hung up the phone and quickly went outside to find Mary.

"Mary, Mary, honey. Listen. We own a light!"

Mary was unemotional upon hearing the news. "This is our dream, honey," Rose continued. "We'll be by water; we'll open a gift shop. We'll make it into a bed and breakfast. Oh, I'm so happy. This is wonderful news, Mary."

Mary didn't respond for several seconds and then said softly, "My friends."

"What about your friends, honey?"

"No more friends for Mary."

"Nonsense, you'll meet lots of people," Rose replied. "You'll have new friends in no time at all."

"My friends bowl, party, dance, go to a movie."

"Yes, yes, I know, honey. But, all of those things will be where we're going."

"I'm not going, Rose."

"I won't hear of such a thing. Of course you are going."

"The word in the puzzle is 'the'."

"What puzzle?"

"The puzzle on your body."

10

Once Lou became involved with the Webberson disappearance, he did what all detectives do — he suspected the family. He knew that four eyes and ears were better than his two, so he asked Jack to accompany him. On Sunday afternoon, July 15, in southeast Michigan, they interviewed Theodore, Florence, and Victoria individually, beginning with Theodore.

Lou had heard of Ted's apparent dementia from Florence when he called to set up his interview. She advised Lou that talking to Ted was a waste of time because he wouldn't have a clue about what was going on. Lou liked the pun, but he decided to talk to Ted anyway. He and Jack registered as guests at the group home. An attendant wheeled Ted into the living room where Lou and Jack waited.

"Theodore? My name is Lou Searing. I'm pleased to meet you. This is my partner, Jack Kelly."

"Nice to meet you two, I guess. What're you selling?" Ted asked.

"We're not selling anything. We're looking into the murder of your brother, and we were hoping you could answer some questions for us."

"Murder of whom?"

"Your brother, Arthur."

"He's dead?" Ted questioned unemotionally. "I outlived him — how about that? Everyone figured I'd be the first in the ground, but old Art beat me. You know, he always had to be first in everything he did, so this doesn't surprise me. What'd he die of?"

"He was murdered," Lou replied.

"Oh, my! What a way to go. Who did it?" Ted asked. "Did they say I did it? Is that why you're here?"

"We don't know who did it, and no one has said you did," Lou replied. "I would like you to answer some questions, which might give us an idea who might have wanted your brother dead."

"I wanted him dead."

"Did you kill him?" Lou inquired.

"Of course not. My crossword buddy killed him. I asked her to. She likes me, said she'd do whatever would make me happy. I told her to kill him and she did."

"Who is your crossword buddy?"

"I'm not telling, and you should know better than to ask me." Ted suddenly became petulant.

"You identified this person as a woman," Lou said.

"I made that up. There's this voice, sort of an imaginary friend who helps me with my crossword puzzles. I see a woman who comes to the home — anyone here will tell you no woman comes here to work on crossword puzzles."

"Either way, you're saying the person who murdered your brother is an imaginary character who visits you and helps you with your crossword puzzles. Have I got that right?"

"Yup. How could I kill my brother? They won't even let me out of here to visit Santa Claus at the town square, let alone to kill someone."

Lou could tell that Ted either suffered from a delusional disorder or was bent on adding confusion to the mix. He thanked Ted for speaking with them, jotted some notes in his spiral notebook, then he and Jack left after signing out.

Once in the car, Lou asked, "Well, what did you make of that, Jack?"

"I liked him."

"OK, but did you get any indication of his role in this?"

"He's sharper than anyone gives him credit for. I think if we dug a little deeper, he might be a key player. If he's not the one who arranged for Arthur's death, he knows more than he indicated."

"Interesting," Lou replied. "My gut reaction was that he's play-ing dominoes while the rest of the world is deep into a game of Bridge, if you know what I mean."

"I disagree. He is one sharp guy, so sharp that he's able to move in and out of where you want him to be. In the long run, this guy will play a key role in this case. Mark my words."

"Fine," Lou said shaking his head. "You're entitled to your opin-ion and I respect that, but my gut says he'll be no help."

Next, Lou and Jack drove over to meet with Florence Webber-son. She was gracious and eager to help Jack and Lou, for she seemed sincere in wanting to know who was responsible for the murder of her husband.

"Thank you for meeting with us, Mrs. Webberson. This is Jack Kelly, my assistant."

"You're welcome. Nice to meet you both. I know this will be solved with precision now that you're on the case, Mr. Searing."

"We'll do our best, Mrs. Webberson."

"Please call me Florence. Can I choose the name you use for me in your next book?"

"My next book?" Lou asked, puzzled by her question.

"You always write a book about the murder you solve, and when you write about this one, I want my character to have a special name. Will you use my suggestion for the character who represents me?"

"Names in my books are given to characters from my imagination. However, if you have a name for me to consider, I'll do so." Lou thought it odd that Florence seemed more interested in her place in his book than securing justice for the murder of her husband. "Do you have any insights that will help me solve Arthur's murder?"

"Not really. Anyone could have done it."

"You don't know anyone who wanted Arthur killed?" Lou asked.

"Well, now that you ask it that way, I suppose the sky's the limit."

"'Sky's the limit'?" Lou repeated the phrase, surprised with Florence's choice of words.

"When you deal in the world of money, really big money, you come to view everyone as a suspect. You see, greed is very powerful. People who don't pay a debt, or fail to follow through on a promise, or people who give bad advice are all suspect."

"That's true for poor people as well," Jack added.

"Yes, I know, but suspicion is multiplied when we are talking about big money. I say this because the resources are handy to pay people to cover up messes, so to speak."

"I see. Are there any skeletons in Arthur's closet?" Lou asked.

"You bet, but you won't learn about them from me," Florence replied. "I'm fairly certain that whoever killed Arthur has nothing to do with his skeletons."

"But you won't expose the skeletons?" Lou pleaded.

"No way will I tell Arthur's secrets. We made promises to one another, and revealing the real Arthur is not going to be a result of his unfortunate death."

"So you believe Arthur is dead?" Jack asked.

"I believe he's gone and won't be seen again. If you mean dead in that fashion, yes, he is dead."

"Thank you. Any questions, Jack?"

"Yes. What name would you like when Lou writes his next novel?"

"Thank you, darling, for asking. I would like my name to be 'Elizabeth Taylor'. And, if Mr. Searing's book becomes a movie, I would like Glenn Close to play my part."

"Well, I'm fairly certain there won't be a movie, Florence," Lou said with a chuckle. "However, I'll consider giving you the name 'Elizabeth Taylor.' But, may I ask why?"

"Why? You don't see a resemblance?" Florence asked, smiling and flashing her diamond ring.

"Forgive me for asking," Lou replied.

"I do think Lou would like a Webberson family picture," Jack interjected. "Do you have a group photo of everyone? Lou could use it when he describes various people in the novel."

"Yes, actually I do. We used the family photo for our Christmas cards last year. I'll get one for you."

"Thank you for your suggestion," Lou said, nodding to Jack. "And, thank you for the photo, ma'am."

The two moved on to Victoria's home. After introductions and a few preliminary remarks, it became clear to Lou and Jack that Arthur's daughter felt no emotion regarding her father. "He was a lousy father, gentlemen. If you ever needed an example of a man totally immersed in himself, it would be my father. My brother Wally is right: everything the man did was conditional. Everything revolved around what was in it for him. I didn't love my father because I never felt love from him."

"That's sad," Jack replied. "I guess money can do that."

"I don't think it was money. I think he simply didn't like anyone under the age of, say, forty. If you were that young, you didn't have money, and if you couldn't play his real-life version of Monopoly, then you had no ticket into my father's life."

"Do you have any idea who might have killed your father?" Lou asked.

"Someone with a ticket who, once they knew him, found Daddy more interested in money than a person or a cause."

"Any idea who meets those criteria?" Jack asked.

"No, because Daddy never allowed us to see that part of his life."

"You inherited ten million from your father's estate, am I correct?" Lou asked.

"Yes."

"Forgive me for asking, but do you consider that fair?" Jack asked.

"I'm lucky I got a dollar," Victoria replied. "I have no idea why I received any money. Maybe it was guilt. Maybe he finally decided that his daughter was deserving of a part of his wealth."

"You expected more?" Lou asked.

"I didn't expect anything. I wasn't part of his life, so why would he give me a dime? But, since he has, I'm grateful. We are fairly well-to-do anyway because my husband is most successful in business. But I support several charities and I plan to pass money along to those who need funds just to meet expenses."

"Thanks for talking with us," Lou said. "Your brother, Wally, has declined my request to talk with him. Is this consistent with your understanding of his personality?"

"It should not surprise you that Wally won't be interviewed. He is not very resourceful and quite honestly, while he is not the brightest apple on the tree, he's smart enough not to find himself in an interview with a couple of intelligent detectives."

Lou and Jack returned to west Michigan, stopping for dinner in Grand Rapids. They realized they hadn't gotten much information from the Webberson family.

"One statement in the three interviews was worth the day," Lou said, studying his notes while his after-dinner coffee cooled. "Any idea what I'm talking about?"

"Probably Victoria's statement that the murderer was someone in Webberson's life who didn't know how to play his game."

"No, I took that as a given. The important statement came from Florence in response to your question, 'Do you think he is dead'?"

"Must not have stuck," Jack replied looking over his notes.

"She said, 'I believe he's gone, never to be seen again. And, if this means dead to you, he's dead'."

"You're right!"

"She referred to secrets you don't share with others, but with that one remark she may have exposed his biggest secret — that he is alive."

A couple of bites of apple pie later, the men had paid their bills and were once again on I-96 heading home.

11

JULY 17 · ARTHUR WEBBERSON'S MEMORIAL SERVICE

Early in the spring, Arthur Webberson had signed up to be an honorary lighthouse keeper at the Big Sable Point Lighthouse. He loved this annual activity; it allowed him to live at a light for a week, to walk the shore of Lake Michigan, and to meet people who were fascinated with lighthouses. It was almost like coming home.

Arthur spent a lot of time at lights in the summer. Like a bishop who moved from parish to parish with a suitcase in tow, Arthur would visit lighthouse after lighthouse, announcing his arrival twenty-four to forty-eight hours in advance. He was always welcome, and wherever he went, the owner or manager would contact the local paper to announce his impending arrival.

Arthur had done more for the popularity of lights in the Great Lakes than any other individual or group of people. He had secured federal funds for the purchase and upkeep of many lights. Arthur had arranged tours to lights before they were popular. He was a founder of the HOMES Lighthouse Association so that the lighthouses could exist on a foundation that was fiscally and programmatically sound. If the lights of the Great Lakes were to have a parade, Arthur Webberson would be the Grand Marshal. He was that popular, and he had been important to the success of lights throughout the Great Lakes.

In 2005 the Michigan Chamber of Commerce named Arthur their Man of the Year. As lighthouse tours became more popular, money flowed into communities where lighthouse fans ate, slept, bought souvenirs, and shopped. Arthur Webberson was not only an influential man and an important cog in the lighthouse machine, he was practically an icon. But notoriety comes with a price. It isn't uncommon for well-known, popular personalities to have enemies. People become jealous, envious, disenchanted with highly-visible personalities, no matter what brings them recognition and power.

Events following the death of Arthur seemed a bit unusual, but true to his personality, everything was carried out as he had directed. There would be no autopsy, no organ donation, merely cremation with a request that his daughter spread his ashes around the Big Sable Lighthouse in Ludington, his favorite.

After family and guests had arrived and taken their seats, Arthur was eulogized in a manner befitting a king. Several people recalled him as a prominent citizen, a successful entrepreneur, a philanthropist, and a man who was respected for his many qualities. There were flowers all around the lighthouse, and there was a somber air about the place. Everyone present gathered to pay their respects to Florence, Wallace, and Virginia. Because there had been a murder, the place was abuzz about who did it and why, as people sought news to satisfy their curiosity.

Julian Hicks, the HOMES Association President, spoke at the memorial service. "To say that Arthur's death has devastated our association and the people who love lighthouses is an understatement. Arthur was an icon in the lighthouse world. He was known to every-one, and his final bequest is not only generous but much appreciated in preservation circles." Other speakers lauded Arthur as a man who had a passion for the lights and who loved the light people as much, if not more, than his family.

Most glances in the direction of the Webberson family came from judgmental minds. It was generally assumed that someone in the family had killed Arthur, and most people were sure of that — they just didn't know who. Wally would have been the top vote getter. Florence didn't need Arthur's money, but she might be put-out not to get a penny. Victoria had received ten million, and while that wasn't much, hers was the only inheritance beyond the pittance Ted received.

Theodore was at the funeral along with Ike and Jenny. Jenny came because she was curious about this nutty family. She had heard of each character and, to her recollection, none of them met with Ted's approval. She also wanted to view Arthur's body. After all, as far as she knew, Ted believed she had murdered the man. She was disappointed to learn after the long trip that there was no body to view, only ashes.

Following the service, Victoria opened the small urn and, thankful for a very calm day, walked round the light sprinkling her father's ashes, stopping once to wipe some tears that had welled up in her eyes and fallen onto her cheeks.

During the reception, one remark resembled a match striking a near open can of gasoline. Ted, Ike, and Jenny sat at a table eating lunch when a man approached Ted and offered his hand in greeting. Ted shook his hand but seemed not to recognize him.

"I'm sorry, my memory isn't very good. I don't remember your name," Ted said.

"I'm Don Miller, Ted. I worked with your brother for many years. I was the one who organized those Canadian fishing excursions he enjoyed so much."

"Oh, yes, Art liked those trips. These are my friends from where I live now, in a group home . This is my friend Ike; I named him after General Dwight David Eisenhower. And this is Jenny Mitchell. She comes to visit me at the home, and she's the one who murdered Art!"

"Hello. Nice to meet... murdered Art? You killed my friend?" Don was shocked.

"Oh, no, that's just Ted being ridiculous," Jenny replied. "Ted misunderstands a lot. Of course I didn't murder your friend."

"You did too!" Ted fired back. "I asked you to kill him and you did it — darn good job too!"

Don was obviously uncomfortable, but Ted and Ike smiled, enjoying the dialogue. Don took a deep breath, turned to Ted and said, "Listen, Ted, nice to see you." Don then turned to Ike and Jenny and said, "Nice meeting you two." They both smiled and shook his hand. Don turned and walked a bit unsteadily into the crowd.

Jenny turned to Ted. "Why did you tell him I killed your brother?"

"People need a little excitement in their lives," Ted replied. "A few minutes ago, Don was mingling with a dull and somber crowd, wanting more to be seen than to mourn. Now, Don has some excitement. He's got a rumor — a story."

"Yeah, but the police will come knocking on my door," Jenny said, shaking her head.

"Then, you'll have some excitement and a story." Ted grinned, and Ike laughed out loud, but Jenny just frowned, shaking her head, and taking a deep breath.

"But, the three of us know it's true," Ted continued. "You killed Art, and I love you for it. You keep your promises, and that virtue will take you a long way in life."

"Yeah, all the way to the gallows, and a shorter life than I had planned on."

Wally and Bea kept to themselves at the service, both very uncomfortable. They knew that every glance in their direction was judgmental. Wally wasn't grieving, for there hadn't been love or bonding with his father. He was at the service because he was expected to be there, and Bea was there to support Wally. Other than a few people who knew Wally as Art's son, nobody took time to greet him.

To date, there was no progress on the Bowman murder in Manistee. Leads were few and nothing seemed to point to a resolution of that case. Lou offered to assist authorities in Manistee, but Chief McFadden, sure the two murders were committed by the same person or persons, encouraged Lou to give his attention to the Webberson murder, thinking Lou's solving that one would solve his case.

12

The day was July 18. It was steamy hot, the kind of day that Lou liked to bask in air conditioning. But on this day there appeared to be a break in the case. Mickey McFadden called Lou and asked him to call Wayne Conn at Two Men and a Truck.

"Mr. Conn? Lou Searing here. Chief McFadden suggested I call you."

"Yes, Mr. Searing. I told the chief one of my men thought he might have some information for you."

"I'm all ears."

"Well, this employee, who doesn't want me to tell you his name, is very interested in lighthouses and is following Mr. Webberson's murder in the media. Anyway, this man was on the crew that moved the Kammeraad Funeral Home in Reed City. They were going about their work when he noticed the name on a body bag, and that name was Webberson. He had heard that the body had been taken to a funeral home, but no one knew which one. So, it could be Kammeraad in Reed City. Is this helpful?"

"Extremely helpful."

"There was quite a bit of confusion with the Webberson body too. We moved four bodies and the funeral home claims there were only three bodies. The name on the tag, 'A. Webberson,' was said often enough that one of my men finally made the connection to the murder."

"Or disappearance," Lou replied, as he still had no proof Arthur was dead. "Thank you for passing along the information. I'll take it from here. Please thank your employee and let him know that I may need to ask him some questions before this case is wrapped up."

"I'm sure he will cooperate — he just doesn't want any attention drawn to himself. I'm sure you understand."

"Yes, I do."

Lou called Jack to brief him and then contacted J.W. Kammeraad, the owner of the funeral home to arrange a meeting. Lou drove to Reed City, found the funeral home, walked in and asked the receptionist if he could see Mr. Kammeraad. He was escorted into a fashionable office, offered a seat, and coffee.

"Thanks for seeing me on short notice," Lou began.

"Service is our highest priority," J.W. said solemnly.

"The Mason County sheriff has asked me to look into the disappearance or possible murder of Arthur Webberson. From what I learned this morning, the deceased might have been brought here?"

"Let me check my records." J.W. looked in his business log and drew his finger down a list of clients. "Yes, as a matter of fact he was. His body was brought here on July 10."

"Who brought the body here?" Lou asked.

"We don't know."

"You don't know?" Lou asked, astonished. "How can that be?"

"A car pulled up at the loading dock in back. The maintenance man, Kenneth James thought the delivery was arranged. He thought the person died in his home, and no one knew what to do, except to bring the body to a funeral home."

"Okay, I see the misunderstanding, but who brought the body?" Lou asked.

"We don't know."

"Man or woman, one person or several?"

"One person, a woman."

"Young, old, fat, thin…"

"From what I understand, middle-aged, 'normal,' whatever that means. The vehicle was a newer model SUV."

"Do you have surveillance cameras outside your entrances?"

"No."

"Okay, so the body was dropped off here. What happened next?" Lou inquired.

"The body was taken to our preparation area downstairs, as is common practice. We then got a call from a supposed attorney, a man telling us that according to Mr. Webberson's estate, he was the proper person to discuss plans for burial. Apparently the will had stated specific plans for the burial, and those plans did not include our funeral home."

"So, you turned the body over to this attorney?"

"No, he didn't give a name, and I can't just take someone's word that he is an attorney. I told him we needed a court order."

"Did he offer to sign any papers, and where is the body now?" Lou asked.

"No, he did not, and the body was turned over to a member of the family."

"When?"

"Ah, let's see. The body was given back to the family on July 12."

"Why did you call the Mason County sheriff when you received the body?"

"I didn't call the sheriff. Who said I did?" J.W. asked.

"The sheriff received a cell phone call saying the body of Arthur Webberson was at a funeral home."

"I certainly didn't make the call. Why would I call the sheriff?"

"That's what I am trying to find out. May I talk with this Mr. James?"

"Yes, you may." J.W. contacted his secretary and directed that Ken James be paged and asked to come to his office. "He should be here shortly. Do you wish a private meeting?"

"Yes, please."

"You can use my office."

"Thank you." While waiting for Mr. James to arrive, Lou wondered how Arthur's attorney, if he did indeed call, knew that Arthur's body was in Reed City.

Kenneth James had been with the funeral home since he was a teen hired to mow the lawn in 1949. He rose to head the maintenance staff, and then retired. But, finding retirement a bore, he returned to the home for part-time work.

"Welcome to your home before the grave, Mr. Searing," Ken said, with a smile and a firm handshake.

"Thank you. Kind of an odd introduction you have there," Lou replied. "It sure hits one up-side the head with a taste of reality."

"Well, yes, but it's a good ice-breaker, or, as we call it in our business, a ground-breaker. People chuckle, and we get off to a comfortable start."

"All downhill from there, right?" Lou asked, trying to add to the humor.

"Yes, but we say, all 'down under' from there."

Lou shook his head at the attempt at humor. "Let me get right to my questions."

"By all means."

"I already understand from Mr. Kammeraad that you thought arrangements had already been made for Mr. Webberson, and so you took the body, correct?"

"Yes, I did."

"Do you know what kind of vehicle the woman who brought the body here was driving?"

"I know it was an SUV, dark, like black or dark green."

"The woman who brought the body — tall, short, beautiful?"

"Nope. She was just a normal-looking woman."

"'Normal' means many things to many people, Mr. James."

"I know, but I mean nothing stood out about her. I guess she was on the heavy side as opposed to skinny, if that helps. She wore sunglasses and a hat."

"Could you pick her out of a lineup?"

"Probably."

Lou brought out the Webberson group photo, showed it to Mr. James and asked, "Do any of these women look like the one who delivered the body?"

"Might have been this one," Kenneth said, pointing at Victoria. "But, then again, maybe not."

"You are sure it was a woman?"

"Yes."

"And, she was alone?"

"I didn't see anyone else in the vehicle."

"How about age — can you estimate that for me?" Lou asked.

"I'm not good at this. She wasn't real young, or real old."

"But if you had to guess, what would you say?"

"If I had to guess, maybe forty. That's just a guess."

"She didn't sign any papers?" Lou asked.

"No. Like I said, I assumed the arrangements had been taken care of. Sorry."

"So, nothing was odd or different about this woman? No birthmarks, scars, unusual hair style?"

"Come to think of it, I suppose there was something different."

"What was that?"

"The vehicle didn't have a proper license plate, just one of those black-on-white signs in the back window — you know, a temporary license. Maybe she just bought the car or something?"

"Thanks. That observation could help. Before I go, did you call the Mason County sheriff to say the body was here?"

"No, I certainly did not."

"If you remember anything else, let me know, okay?" Lou handed him a business card.

"Sure. Sorry I wasn't more observant."

Lou wanted more information about the Webberson body. He asked to see Mr. Kammeraad before leaving, and the two men met in Mr. Kammeraad's office. "I talked to Mr. Conn of Two Men and a Truck, and he says there is confusion about a body being moved to your new facility," Lou began.

"Yes, that's true. We didn't complain, but we don't know how this miscommunication occurred. I would like my assistant Lisa Colby to join us. She's responsible for record keeping and can answer your questions better than I."

"By all means."

J.W. picked up the phone, paged his assistant, and asked that she join them in his office. Within a minute Lisa arrived and sat down in front of the desk.

"Thank you for joining us, Lisa. Mr. Searing is assisting the Mason County sheriff in investigating the death of Arthur Webberson, one of our customers."

"Hello," Lisa said with a smile.

Lou nodded and returned the smile.

"You have some questions, Mr. Searing," J.W. said. "Please proceed."

"Thank you. I'd like to clear up the confusion about the body of Mr. Webberson. Do you know anything about this?"

"Mr. Webberson's body was one of four that were to be moved to this parlor," Lisa began. "However, when his daughter asked to have possession of the body, the inventory was changed to show three bodies to be moved. If the Two Men and a Truck Company told you

117

there were four bodies moved, they were mistaken. Three bodies were loaded into their truck and three bodies were transferred from the truck to our new preparation laboratory."

"So, Arthur's daughter asked for his body, and you released his body to her?"

"That is correct."

"That's acceptable?" Lou asked. "I mean can you legally as well as ethically release a corpse to the family?"

"It seldom happens, but nothing prohibits the family from taking the remains," J.W. explained.

"That's certainly unusual," Lou offered shaking his head.

"We violated no law," Mr. Kammeraad replied. "I will admit it seems unconventional, but they are customers, and as with any business, if they want the body, we give it to them. We give them the ashes when they request them, so we give them the whole body if they request it."

"And if I might ask, why would you transfer bodies via a moving company? This funeral home seems like a class place, so, why wouldn't you transfer the bodies in your hearse?"

"Mr. Searing. I don't need to tell you how to solve a crime, and likewise, I don't wish for you to tell me how to run my business. We are not talking about moving patients from a nursing home. The matter is dead, no different than a chair."

"I agree it's not my place to suggest how you do your business, but I would certainly not want my mother being shipped in a Two Men and a Truck moving van."

"I can assure you that our families do not know how their relative is 'shipped' as you say. They trust us to move the body carefully and we do. We have great confidence in Two Men and a Truck."

Lou jotted a few notes and thanked both Mr. Kammeraad and Lisa for responding to his questions. Before leaving the funeral home parking lot, he called Two Men and a Truck and asked to speak to Mr. Conn.

"Mr. Searing. How can I help you today?"

"I just spoke with the funeral home folks. They say you only took three bodies to the new funeral home even though your inventory recorded four bodies."

"Whoa, whoa, whoa. You're getting me pretty upset here, Lou."

"I'm just trying to learn the truth."

"And I'm telling you the truth," Wayne replied. "I note on my load sheet exactly what goes on the truck and what comes off the truck. Four bodies went on the truck, Mr. Searing."

"Did you see each body?"

"No, not the actual body. You see, well, let me try to explain. Each body was on a metal cart, or gurney, or whatever they're called. The body is in a body bag, and there is an ID tag attached to the bag. My men put four of those bags on the truck. I may not be able to do a lot of things, but counting to four is something I can handle."

"Ok, so four on, and four off?"

"That's right. Four on, and four off. Now, there could have been potatoes in the bags for all I know. I didn't see the actual bodies, but each bag on the cart weighed about the same and it appeared that a body was in each bag, and each bag had a tag with a name."

"But I'm told by the funeral home folks that three bodies went on and three came off," Lou repeated.

"You are getting the truth from me, Lou. We put four body bags on the truck, and we took four body bags off the truck. The funeral home can claim anything they want, but my men and I know the truth — four on, and four off. And, you know something else? The funeral home has not said one word to us about this. They haven't filed a complaint or contacted us for an explanation. We're happy. They're happy. Who's not happy?"

"Me," Lou replied.

Still in his car in the funeral home parking lot, Lou called Victoria.

"Victoria, this is Lou Searing. I'm looking into your father's death."

"Oh, yes, Mr. Searing."

"Maybe you can clear up a mystery for me."

"Hmmm, sort of turning the tables here, aren't you?"

"Meaning?"

"Well, aren't you the one who solves mysteries?" Victoria asked.

"Yes, but without sufficient facts, I can't do my job."

"I'll help if I can."

"Did you ask to take possession of your father's body from the Kammeraad Funeral Home in Reed City?"

"No."

"No?"

"Of course not. Why would I want his body?" Victoria asked.

"The funeral home people say you requested the body and took your father's remains from the funeral home before their move."

"Preposterous! They're trying to cover up something. I mean, maybe they have me confused with someone else, but no, I did not take Dad's remains from the home."

"Thank you."

Lou walked back to the funeral home and sought out both Mr. Kammeraad and Lisa.

"In the last fifteen minutes I have talked to the Two Men and a Truck supervisor and to Mr. Webberson's daughter. The supervisor says he and his men put four body bags onto their truck and took four off at your new facility. The daughter says she did not come here and claim her father's remains."

"I think I finally figured out the confusion. The supervisor is telling the truth, and the daughter is lying," Mr. Kammeraad said emphatically.

"Please explain."

"Gladly. After the daughter took Mr. Webberson's body, we did not remove the tag from the bag, and my staff may have put laboratory items in the bag, knowing it was going to be moved here. In fact, that might explain it. One moment please." J.W. Kammeraad lifted the phone off the cradle, punched an extension number. "Chris, when the move took place, did you or Eric put items from your lab in the body bag where Mr. Webberson had previously been held?" After a slight pause, J.W. said, "I thought so. Thanks." J.W. turned to Lou, "Yes, that's what happened."

"Ok, let me see if I have this," Lou summarized. "Four bags on, and four bags off — three bodies, and one bag of supplies or materials. Mr. Webberson's body was taken earlier by Victoria. So, Victoria is lying."

"That's correct."

"Do you have any papers to document the transfer?"

"Certainly. Today, everything needs to be documented."

"May I see the release-of-body paperwork?" Lou asked.

"I need to get it," J.W. stated. "I'll be right back."

Within a minute, Mr. Kammeraad was back to Lou. "Here is a copy for you."

"Thanks." Lou looked at the signature. He saw, "Alice Livernois."

As Lou drove out of Reed City he called Jack to report what he had learned. "We have a new suspect, Alice Livernois."

"That's odd," Jack replied. "Could be the murderer, Lou."

"Or, could be a co-conspirator in deception."

13

Lou received an e-mail:

Mr. Searing: My summer school students at Greenville High School love your books. We've been following the case of the Lighthouse Murders in our local paper and would like to help you solve it. We know this sounds odd, for a whole class to be involved, but we like to think we're smart and creative. Can you use our help?

It was signed, Mrs. Bell and Students.

Lou pondered; his initial thought was to thank Mrs. Bell, but pointing out it was next to impossible for an entire class to become involved. Just the logistics would be a nightmare not to mention liability concerns and protection of confidential information. Then Lou thought better of his negative response. If two heads were better than one, what might twenty heads do? He changed his mind and called Mrs. Bell to accept her offer.

The next day Lou went to Greenville High School and explained his requirements to the students. They agreed to his terms and soon the classroom turned into a "situation room." Files were set up and a map of Michigan was tacked to the bulletin board, ready for colorful pins to denote strategic settings or moves in the investigation.

Mrs. Bell divided the students into four groups. One group would be on-site people who would travel with Lou or Jack, if appropriate. A second group would analyze information. A third group would catalog evidence, and the fourth would research and follow leads when Lou requested assistance..

Finally, two students in the class volunteered to work with Lou on a book about the case after the fact, for Lou always wrote up his cases in a novel. Ethan Bean and Rebekah Grimm had no interest in crime-solving, but they were quite interested in writing up the case.

Lou talked with the Greenville High School principal who then set up a conference call with the superintendent. The three agreed the experience would be positive as long as the possibility of any student coming into harm's way would be practically impossible. While Lou couldn't guarantee total safety, he expected that students would be resource people at best, able to follow the excitement of the investigation, but far removed from any confrontation. In addition, any travel away from school related to his project would require school and parent permission.

Lou was finally able to convince Wallace Webberson to talk with him. "Thank you for meeting with me, Wallace."

"Call me Wally. I've decided to do whatever I can to be helpful, Mr. Searing."

"Thank you."

"I'm certain fingers are being pointed directly at me. My family knows how upset I was after Dad explained his will; the two of us have been estranged for a long time. My friends know how angry I am, and the idea of revenge no doubt entered their minds. I mean, if I didn't know that I was innocent, I would be pointing the guilty finger at myself — convinced that this is an open-and-shut case of murder — father and son rivalry: son spurned in will, son kills father."

"Did 'son kill father'?" Lou asked.

"No, Mr. Searing, and a thousand times no. I'd pass any lie detector test. I can prove my whereabouts when he died, and you can speak to my attorney who advised me in no uncertain terms that it was in my best interests that my father remain alive."

"'Remain alive'? You mean you talked to your attorney about killing him?"

"No, no, no. I talked to him about strategies for obtaining what I thought — and still think — is a justified inheritance. My attorney said I should do whatever I could to make sure my father lived, because if he died, the will would be legal and changing it would be next to impossible."

"I'd like your whereabouts around the time your father died," Lou said, looking over his notes.

"Not a problem."

"If you didn't do it, who did?"

"You know, I've given that a lot of thought. I haven't any idea."

"Who could have done it?" Lou asked.

"Well, when you have as much money as Dad had, or has, as the case may be, a lot of people gather around you claiming love and affection. There are some who are resentful, jealous, or maybe even feel spurned."

"Let me get to the point," Lou said. "Did he gamble? Did he deal in drugs? Did he have debts? Did he have a revengeful mistress? Or, did someone owe your father a lot of money and kill him to cancel the debt? The list goes on and on. Do my questions bring any names to mind?"

"Dad didn't gamble, he didn't deal in drugs. He certainly never had a debt that I know of. Yes, people owed him money, but he never loaned huge amounts of money, so I doubt that's the case. An upset mistress? Not that I am aware of. My dad was respected and feared, Mr. Searing. He chose his friends wisely. He was very successful in managing his money. He gave to worthy causes. The only one who would have a motive to kill him, in my mind anyway, is me."

"And did you do it?" Lou asked point-blank.

"I most certainly did not."

Lou was intrigued by Jenny Mitchell, Ted's crossword puzzle friend. He decided to talk with her, so arranged to meet her for lunch at the Cottage Inn Restaurant in Ann Arbor.

After cordial greetings, Lou began. "Thanks for meeting with me."

"Sure. I don't think I've ever met a detective before. Well, I guess I have, in that I've been interviewed by the sheriff up in Mason County. You don't look like a detective, Mr. Searing."

"What's a detective supposed to look like?"

"Moustache, dark jacket, hair, sneaky expression…"

"Hair?" Lou replied, smiling.

"Well, you know, Colombo, James Bond, Perry Mason, Boston Blackie — they all had hair."

"Boston Blackie. That name that hasn't come up in a long time. Most don't remember it, but I remember sitting in front of my parents' black-and-white Raytheon TV and watching that show. How would a youngster like you know about Boston Blackie?" Lou asked.

"My dad is a mystery nut. He collects old-time radio and TV shows. I sit with him on occasion and watch old shows or clips from shows. I liked Boston Blackie and that little dog he had with him. That's another thing you detectives are supposed to have — a dog."

"I have a dog, but she stays home."

"Anyway, you are a detective, so how can I help you?"

"As you know, you are a suspect in Arthur Webberson's death or disappearance, and…"

"Yeah, but it's ridiculous and you must know that."

"Well, it doesn't help when Theodore tells the world that you killed Mr. Webberson, and you enjoy crossword puzzles, and an unfinished crossword puzzle sits near where he reportedly died."

"I'll tell you what I told the sheriff so you two will be on the same page," Jenny began. "I need practicum hours for my course in geriatrics. So, I go to the group home and meet Ted and Ike. They are easy to talk to, Ted likes crossword puzzles as do I, and we share the fun. I told Ted if he ever needed me to do anything for him, to let me know. So, one day he reminded me of this and asked me to kill his brother. I said, 'Ok, how and when, and who is he?' He seemed a bit surprised that I would kill for him, but he gave me the information and he still believes I killed Arthur."

"Did you?"

"Of course not. Think about this for a minute, Mr. Searing. Why would I kill someone and subject myself to a life of incarceration for an old man in a group home? I'm a student, earning hours for a course. My professor lectures on common characteristics of the elderly — losing touch with reality, fantasy thoughts, and unrealistic perceptions of situations. I'm told that the best way to respond to these expressions is to go along with them. There's no sense explaining reality, because these folks don't live there. There's no sense in arguing, because they're convinced they're right. So, I said, 'OK, I'll kill him'."

"In retrospect, you probably wish you hadn't agreed to honor his wish."

"Probably. But on the other hand, it's interesting to watch how the police, attorneys, detectives, and others investigate a crime. It's like walking onto the set of *CSI: Miami* and getting to play a part, even though my part is of an outlandish red herring."

"Where were you the day of the murder?" Lou asked.

"You can't be serious! You're really going to look into this as if I may have killed some guy?"

"I'm just clearing people, Jenny. The more I see a piece that doesn't fit the puzzle, the more comfortable I am putting that piece to the side."

"I think I remember from the newspaper and the sheriff's interview that he was murdered on July 10, a Saturday. On Monday I have two classes, and both have major tests on Mondays. So, I spend most Saturday afternoons and evenings at the library."

"Which library?"

"The main library on the EMU campus."

"Ok, go on."

"Let's see… Saturday evening for dinner, I usually get a sandwich at Subway. Then, about nine or so, I go to my apartment and try to get some sleep. That was my day."

"You don't go home for the weekend, wherever that is?" Lou asked.

"No, that's Stockbridge, Michigan, by the way."

"What knowledge do you have of poisons?" Lou asked.

"Poisons? Well, if something has a skull and crossbones on it, it's poison; or if the can is full of pesticides, it's poison. I don't know any more than anyone typically would."

"Never had a class in it?"

"In poisons? Of course not! You think I'm a pervert or something? I hate chemistry. I'm in a service profession, not aspiring to work for Chem Lawn."

"No need to get defensive," Lou replied. "If you watched Boston Blackie, you saw he always asked questions."

"Yes, but logical ones. The fact that you are even talking to me is illogical."

"It's routine. Jenny, I waste a lot of time talking to people, but I have a checklist with lots of names on it, and the more information I get, the more lines I draw through names, and I don't give it a second thought. If something doesn't sit right, I keep the name on the list."

"Where am I — about to be crossed off?"

"Actually, no, you remain on the list."

"Give me a break!" Jenny said, shaking her head.

"Jenny, you did not go to the library the afternoon or evening of Saturday, July 10. You took a course in chemistry titled, 'Medications and Their Effect on the Elderly.' And the title of your paper was, *Dangerous Interactions Among Medications Commonly Used by the Elderly.* You got an 'A,' so at least the professor believes you did a good job."

Jenny sat with her head down and didn't say a word.

After several seconds of silence Lou said, "Not your best interview, Jenny. I do my homework too."

"Can I go now?" Jenny said.

"Yes. Thanks for your time. I'll be in touch."

Jenny rose and walked from the restaurant.

The next day, Jenny made an appointment to talk with her academic advisor. She could trust him and had sought fatherly advice from him before. He could see her right away which was comforting.

"You need a couple of ears or a shoulder to cry on, I take it," said Dr. Mange.

"No crying yet, but those listening ears would be most appreciated."

"As the saying goes, 'I'm all ears.' What is on your mind?"

"I've gotten myself into a jam, and if I don't handle it well, I'm going to keep getting deeper and deeper into a mess that is ugly at best, and down right life-changing at worst."

"Sounds pretty serious to me."

"It is," Jenny assured her counselor. "Guess I'll just lay it on you."

"Sure. I'll ask if something isn't logical or sequential."

"As you know, I am taking Geriatrics from Dr. Herbert. One of the requirements is fifty hours of practicum, helping out in a senior center, nursing home, or group home. I chose the group home in Bloomfield Township. There is a man there that I like, by the name of Ted. He likes crossword puzzles, and so do I, so my two hours there twice a week go quickly. And, it easily satisfies that requirement for the class."

"So far, no problem."

"Yes, but here is the problem. In a moment of connecting with the client, I said, 'If there is anything you want me to do for you, just let me know and I'd be glad to help.' This was sincere, because I liked Ted, and what more could he want than picking up some Juicy Fruit Gum at the Seven Eleven?"

"He wanted more than gum. Am I jumping ahead?" Dr. Mange asked.

"Much more. He wanted me to kill his multi-millionaire brother."

"That's a tall order."

"So, to fulfill my promise, I said something to the effect of 'No problem — who, where, when and how?' Ted gave me the answers, and I said I'd do it."

"You did?" Dr. Mange asked, quite surprised at what he had heard.

"Well, I had been taught in a recent lecture that many older people live in a fantasy world, have delusions, make nonsensical statements, and that it's often easier for friends and family members to go along with the irrational comment than to argue or try to correct the error."

"That's true."

"Well, it turns out the brother was supposedly murdered and the police found a crossword puzzle near the body."

"Oh-oh."

"Yup, and then I take Ted to his brother's funeral, and at the reception he introduces me to a friend of his dead brother and saying, 'This is Jenny Mitchell. She killed Arthur'."

"Oh, no."

"Of course, I say, 'Don't be ridiculous,' but he just passes it off. Now, a detective knocks on my door. He's not with the police — he's a private detective of some kind. He asks me lots of logical questions, like, where was I the day of the murder?"

"You told him?" Dr. Mange asked.

"Yeah, I told him my Saturday schedule, but little did I know that he had researched this all out and knew that I wasn't where I said I was on that day. So, now I'm a suspect and a liar. One of his questions was, 'Do you have any knowledge of poisons?' I said, 'Of course not.' But, apparently he had looked into my course work and papers and knew that I had written a term paper on drug interactions and seniors."

"Yup, getting deeper and deeper here," Dr. Mange surmised.

"I just clammed up and asked to leave, which was my right. But I realized that I didn't look good. The next morning, the police arrived and wanted to talk to me. I said I would need an attorney present, so that was arranged. I told them the truth which was that I had spent the day at a state park."

"Good."

"No, not good, because the state park is in Ludington which is where the brother was murdered. So, now I'm in the actual locale of the crime."

"Ouch. Your attorney is helping, I presume."

"I have a meeting with him to go over in more detail what I am telling you, but it seems like every time I open my mouth I get deeper into this crazy world. It's getting to me and I can tell I'm going to need counseling of some kind."

"Well, it seems to me that you are doing the right things: telling the truth, having an attorney present, talking to me, etcetera. My advice is to stay the course you are on. I think I would change your practicum if possible. Simply explain to Ted that the term is over and you have other responsibilities. Does that help?"

"Sure. Thanks for listening. Oh, one more thing. I recently came into some money, a lot of money, like a half-million dollars. Is this going to raise even more questions?"

"I'm sure it will. But, before you go, why did you lie to the detective when he asked about your weekend activities?"

"I was in a very stressful situation, and it just came out, I guess. People do strange things in stressful situations, as you know."

Dr. Mange listened and nodded.

As soon as news of Arthur's murder was announced, Sally Wind-sand, member of the HOMES Board of Directors, had a flashback to the last board meeting when Norman Root told her he would do what he could to get the money to the association before Arthur's natural death. She didn't want to accuse Norman outright of murder, but on the other hand, how obvious could it be? After several days of wondering whether she should contact Mr. Hicks, she decided to call. She respected his manner in handling difficult situations that had arisen in the past.

"Mrs. Windsand?"

"Yes, Julian. I'm surprised you recognized my voice."

"Well, each board member has called me to express either great sadness at the passing of Arthur or great joy at the inheritance we shall now enjoy. I knew I would hear from you and a couple others, so actually I was anticipating your call."

"I have a new category in addition to expressing great sadness and joy. I wish to add, I think I know 'whodunit'."

"Well, I'm not with the police, as you know, and quite frankly, I would rather stick to the established categories of sadness and joy."

"Yes, I can imagine, but I need your advice. At the last board meeting, when you read the letter announcing the inheritance from Arthur, Norman Root leaned over and whispered that he would like to do something to speed that along."

"Yes, yes, I know. He said the same thing to me. Norm was joking; believe me, there was nothing serious about his comments whatsoever! He has been an acquaintance for many years and this is pure nonsense. He is forever making inappropriate comments and they simply go in one ear and out the other."

"But, what should I do?" Sally asked. "Do I call the police? Do I tell Norm I am calling the police? If I don't do anything, I may be withholding evidence, and I could go to jail."

"You will not go to jail, Mrs. Windsand. I am certain the authorities will contact me concerning Arthur's death. I will report the jest with which Mr. Root responded to the letter. If the police wish to take that as something worth looking into, so be it. I see no need for you to interject yourself into the situation, and quite frankly, I would like all members of the board to stay as far away from the investigation as possible. This is a time for all of us to remain low-key and out of the spotlight."

"Okay, if you are going to tell the police about Mr. Root's comment, that's fine with me. I'll stay out of it."

"Thank you, Sally."

"By the way, where was Mr. Root when Arthur was killed?" Sally asked.

"Mrs. Windsand, there you go — worrying again. Please busy yourself with something more important to the planet than Mr. Root's whereabouts. Please, for the good of the association?"

"Ok, but until this is solved, I'll keep hearing Norm's comment, and between you and me, I just wouldn't put it past Mr. Root to bring us some much needed cash. But, I asked for your advice, and I shall follow it."

"Thank you for calling, Sally. Good day."

Coincidentally, while Mrs. Windsand was calling Mr. Hicks, Mr. Root was recalling his comment, certain that the police would come knocking on his door very shortly. He made copious notes to explain his whereabouts every moment of the days either side of Arthur's murder.

Mr. Root also called his lawyer. "Moylan, Johnson, and Feese. To whom may I direct your call?"

"I'd like to speak with Mrs. Margaret Johnson, please."

"May I ask who is calling?"

"Yes, Norm Root."

"One moment."

Margaret answered presently. "Good afternoon, Norman. How can I help you today?"

"I imagine you've heard about the death of Mr. Arthur S. Webberson of Bloomfield Hills?"

"The lighthouse aficionado?" Margaret asked.

"Yes. I'm likely to be a suspect in his murder, so I am calling to alert you, and to seek your counsel."

"Why would you be a suspect?" Mrs. Johnson asked.

"Mr. Webberson bequeathed millions to the HOMES Lighthouse Association. At our last Board meeting a letter from Arthur Webberson's attorney regarding this bequest was read by our president. I whispered to another board member that I would see if I could hasten the money coming to us. She seemed quite disturbed that I would make such a comment."

"Likewise."

"I know, but 'tis me — what can I say?" Norman asked.

"Most of the time, saying nothing would be helpful," Margaret replied sharply.

"It is hard to teach an old dog new tricks."

"Or in your case, Norman, any trick becomes impossible."

"I hear you smiling, Margaret. Anyway, I have documented every minute of my time from the day before through the day following the murder."

"That makes sense, but first as your attorney, I must ask, did you kill this man?"

"Not directly."

"What's that supposed to mean? You hired a hit-man or perhaps set a trap?"

"No, nothing like that. In addition to my irresponsible comment to a fellow board member, I repeated it to Arthur himself; he didn't see my comment as a threat, but he clearly planned to record my remark for safe keeping in the event of his demise."

"A very smart thing to do. This means that I should be receiving a call from either Mr. Webberson's attorney or the police. My advice to you, Mr. Root, is to begin to practice what is virtually impossible for you: keep your mouth shut, and yes, account for every activity in that forty-eight-hour time span."

"I've done that, but there is one problem."

"What pray tell is that?" Attorney Johnson asked.

"There is no one who can vouch for what I have written."

"Great news, Norman, simply wonderful news," Margaret sighed. "We'll be in touch."

Arthur Webberson's attorney, William Scott, had predicted the calamities surrounding his untimely death, cautioning Arthur against a number of things. First and foremost was Arthur's announcement of his intentions to his family. Human nature being what it is, William knew that this would trigger emotions like jealousy, anger, resentment, and envy, to name a few. Then he urged Arthur not to direct a letter to the HOMES Lighthouse Association for similar reasons, but primarily so that the association would not overdo words of praise. One never knows what might happen to money, given the world economy and, while at the time of the letter Arthur was worth millions, no one knew about tomorrow.

But Arthur would hear none of it. He wanted his family to know his plan, and if emotions were expressed, so be it. He wanted the HOMES Lighthouse Association to know of his affection for its purpose, and any appreciation they wished to show was fine with him.

Another strong suggestion that Arthur failed to take was the hiring of a bodyguard. Mr. Scott knew that confusion and bitterness would arise from a family meeting, and it certainly wouldn't hurt to have an impartial observer present, preferably a strong one with defensive capabilities. But, Arthur found it all hog-wash. And so, there was no bodyguard.

Arthur would not hear Attorney Scott say, "I told you so!" but he was right in every way.

As he drove back to Grand Haven, Lou called Jack and explained the role of the Greenville High School students. "Have you got time to go with them to Squaw Island, Jack?"

"Yes. I can work that out."

"Good. Mrs. Bell is an excellent teacher, and they will have adults with them. But I would be much more comfortable if you were along, helping them to help us, if you know what I mean?"

"I do, and I'll enjoy going along."

"Good. We can be in touch by cell phone. Have you got a way to get over to the island?"

"I recommend we leave from Charlevoix. A good friend has a thirty-five-foot yacht which should carry several students and a few adults."

"Wonderful. Who is this friend?"

"John Tromp — we've been friends for a long time. He likes your books too, Lou. If he's available, I know he would enjoy helping out."

"Great. Give him a call. I'll give you Mrs. Bell's phone number and explain that I want you along. Then I'll leave it up to the two of you to work out arrangements. I'll make it clear to Mrs. Bell that you are the contact for the two of us."

"I'll do the best I can."

"I know you will. I'm counting on you."

Jack asked John Tromp about taking some students and a teacher to Squaw Island for a day trip.

"Be glad to. When do you want to go?"

"I haven't talked to the teacher yet, but I would imagine next week. I'll get back to you with a specific date."

"You find out when we need to go, and barring bad weather, we'll get these folks to Squaw Island."

"Thanks. As I recall, you've been looking for some excitement in your life."

"A boat trip to Squaw Island is often enough excitement for me. It can be treacherous, Jack. What makes it a hard voyage sometimes is that you are traveling in a northwest direction while the wind, and there usually is wind on Lake Michigan, is often out of the west or the north. More often than not it feels like you're on a bucking bronco at a rodeo."

Once the students were involved, Lou asked them to research the historical aspect of the Squaw Island Lighthouse. Amid the excitement of working with Mr. Searing, Mrs. Bell obtained parental permission for five students to sail to Squaw Island to learn as much as they could about the light. The principal of the school loaned his recreational vehicle to the students for a week, to set up in a state park. Each night the students would draw straws to see who would get to spend the night in the RV. The others would sleep in tents.

Mrs. Bell and Ms. Scheiern made it clear that this was a school project involving economics, geography, self-help skills, and language arts. The kids would have fun but it wasn't a vacation. Meals were to be planned, food purchased and prepared, and each meal had a clean-up crew.

Except for going up and back, there would be no DVDs, no iPods, or video-games. Once in Charlevoix, the students could read, talk, or exercise, but there would be no access to television or video games. They would take a lap-top on the trip, but only because the Internet might provide relevant information.

The class would visit a few lighthouses in the northwestern part of the Lower Peninsula. Mrs. Bell had collected a variety of books on the northern portion of the Lower Peninsula, its history, people, and economic development. There were also books about lighthouses and Great Lakes shipping.

The students held a number of car washes to raise money for the trip. Justin Aylsworth, who was on the football team, sold chances on an autographed Bret Favre football. The Greenville High School football coach, who used to play football with Bart Starr, was able to arrange for the autographed football. At ten dollars a ticket, this effort alone raised more than two thousand dollars for the trip.

Students James Hopkins, Jordan Cliff, and Michelle Barber, held an auction with items donated by Greenville retailers, raising sixteen hundred dollars. They received donations from several anonymous citizens, and from the Greenville Kiwanis Club. Finally, with funds assured and duffel bags packed, the eighteen students, four parent chaperons, and teachers Ms. Scheiern and Mrs. Bell left for Charlevoix early the morning of July 22. Many students, parents and a reporter and photographer from the *Greenville Daily News* were there to see them off.

Lou had made it clear that the students were to work with his assistant, Jack Kelly, to learn as much as possible about the Squaw Island murder and to report to him by cell phone or e-mail. He expected a detailed written report at the end of the trip.

The students took this opportunity seriously. Two of them had never been outside of Montcalm County, while others had had a variety of travel experiences. Some had gone camping, but most had not. Nobody had sailed to an island in Lake Michigan on a yacht, so everyone was very excited about this opoportunity.

In advance of the trip, the students were required to read at least three books about the area they were visiting. Each student read about the Squaw Island Lighthouse in Jerry Roach's book titled, *The Ultimate Guide to West Michigan Lighthouses*. They learned that The Squaw Island Lighthouse was erected in 1867, to guide ships around a series of islands in the middle of upper Lake Michigan, especially in times of great storms. The original keepers, the Hoffmeister Family, lived at Squaw Island from 1867-1888.

At the time of the murder in 1925, the lighthouse was home to the Edwards family. The keeper, his wife, and their two children, Joseph and Roberta, lived in the lighthouse. Federal and state investigators indicate that Mr. Edwards had discovered some buried treasure and was left for dead while the murderer(s) dragged the chest of gold down the beach, escaping in a boat. The murder was never solved. The family left the island following the murder. Mrs. Edwards went into mourning and died in 1928, a lonely, depressed woman. Joseph loved the sea and joined the Merchant Marine after graduating from the Maritime Academy in Philadelphia. Eventually he sailed around the world. Roberta, at age 16 moved to New York where she became an operatic diva. She moved to Denmark and married a wealthy businessman.

The Squaw Island Lighthouse never had another keeper. Citizens of Beaver Island occasionally tended to the light, but the murder was enough to deter even the most stout-hearted from living in what was thought to be a haunted light. Since 1925 the light had been the subject of numerous ghost stories. Some folks maintain Mr. Edwards still lives in this light, while others shake their heads and say it's all people's imagination.

"Will we be able to go inside this light?" Kim Barber asked.

"No; we asked, but the Coast Guard does not allow anyone inside," Mrs. Bell replied. "Liability is a problem, and it's not a healthy place, given the birds and the variety of other animals that have inhabited the place over the years."

"How can we be investigating this for Mr. Searing if we don't act like investigators? Don't we need to look around inside?" Steve Koonce asked.

"We'll learn a lot about this place, but wandering around inside is not an option."

"I say we cut the deck," Ashley Johnson suggested.

"What does that mean?" Mrs. Bell asked.

"It means we should go in," Ashley replied. "If a murder took place here, and if, as Mr. Searing thinks, there could be some connection, I think we need to look around."

"I agree with Ashley," Stephanie Stump said. "I hope we're not going up there just to look at the outside. We've seen a picture in Mr. Roach's book. I think we need to get our hands dirty."

"Wait a minute, guys," Nichole Hemmingsen said. "We'll do what Mr. Kelly allows us to do."

"Well, I can't imagine him not wanting us to go in. We certainly won't find anything if we don't go in," Stephanie insisted.

"But we don't have permission," Mrs. Bell said emphatically.

"I don't think that should stop us," Gabe Bruning said.

"No one goes into this light unless I say it is okay to do so," Mrs. Bell replied, putting her foot down. "I promise I'll ask around. If we go in, we'll do it legally, and with Mr. Kelly's permission. The last thing I need — or the principal needs, or Greenville needs — is a bunch of our kids breaking laws in another community."

"She's right, Gabe," Nicole replied. "Mrs. Bell knows we think it's important, and she'll do her best to get us in. Let it go." Everyone nodded, and Mrs. Bell was relieved.

"Okay, then, who was assigned the history of this place?" Mrs. Bell asked.

Two arms went into the air. "That's right, Andrew Hinman and William Jackson. Once we get to Charlevoix and have some lunch, let's find the library, so you two can become acquainted with the librarian and get to work."

"What are you thinking so hard about, Andrew?" Ryan Zoerman asked.

"Just wondering what Mr. Searing would do," Andrew replied.

"We ought to get some plastic bracelets, WWLD," Ryan suggested, laughing. "What Would Lou Do."

Andy countered with a thumbs-up sign. "I agree; if Lou Searing were there, what would he do? What would he look for? Who would he talk to? What's important?"

"Mrs. Bell didn't put *How to be a Private Investigator* on our reading list," Ryan said. "We should have asked Mr. Searing what he expects us to do," Steve said.

"I did ask him," Ethan replied.

"And?"

"And, he said two words: 'solve it'."

"'Solve it'? That's it? Give me a break," Steve replied. "We're kids from a high school. Does he think we go to CSI Prep School or something?"

"Maybe he doesn't know what he expects," Ethan said. "I guess you use common sense, follow your gut, and one question leads to another. What more can we do?"

"Guess so."

"The next best thing to having Mr. Searing with us is having Mr. Kelly with us. He'll know what to do," Ryan explained.

Jack stopped in at school to meet Mrs. Bell and go over the trip.

"I'm so glad you're here," Mrs. Bell said with a tone of relief in her voice. "We have lots of interest, but we really aren't sure how to begin. I want the students to dare to take risks and to problem solve, but I'm so thankful that Mr. Searing asked you to be with us."

"I'm happy to be here, but I like your attitude about giving the students the problem solving skills and the freedom to do what is logical."

"They want so much to help Mr. Searing," Mrs. Bell explained. "Said another way, they will be very disappointed if we leave there without something that will help you two solve this thing."

"I understand, but they need to know that the reality of investigating crime is often chasing after nothing. It's part of the process. Knowing what we can lay to rest is often as important as finding the key to a mystery. So, we often can't solve anything without going on the false runs."

"That's an important lesson for the kids. Maybe you could explain that with a few examples the first evening in Charlevoix?"

"Be glad to," Jack replied. "I suggest we allow the students to explore and follow their instincts. If there are questions or situations where you want my advice, just ask. You know, I think I'll spend time looking for clues myself. If I find something of interest, I'll lead the students to it. They need the joy of coming upon something new much more than I do."

"That would be wonderful, Mr. Kelly," Mrs. Bell replied, feeling much more comfortable about the expedition.

14

Lou asked Julian Hicks, president and chairman of the HOMES Lighthouse Association, if Arthur had had enemies, or if Julian knew of anyone who wouldn't cry a tear over Webberson's demise. True to his word to Sally, Julian said, "We have a board member who made an offhand comment to another member. When I announced that millions of Arthur's estate would come to our association upon his passing, this gentleman said words to the effect that he'd do what he could to see that we got that money sooner than planned. Now, Mr. Searing, I'd bet that this man was just saying this in jest. But who knows? He might have meant it. Never in my wildest dreams would I believe it of him, but I suppose there are lots of instances of sweet little old grandmothers knocking off people they don't like."

"Who is this member, and how can I contact him?" Lou asked.

"His name is Norman Root, and his address is... I have it right here, because I know your reputation, and I know you'd want to check him out."

"Thank you, I think."

"Yes, I meant it as a compliment. The other person who comes to mind is a huge fan of lights. In fact her dream is to own one. Her name is Rose McCracken, and she lives with a sister who is mentally retarded or impaired, or whatever words are correct these days.

She lives in Alma, but I don't have her address. Arthur was able to pull strings so that everyday citizens couldn't obtain a light."

"Do you know Rose's sister's name?"

"Yes, her name is Mary. She works part-time at Alma College. They are always together so that on the lighthouse tours, they are often referred to as RoseMary."

"Same last name, I take it?"

"Yes, I believe so."

Lou decided to talk with Mary before speaking with Rose. His background in special education gave him knowledge of organizations that existed to assist children and adults with various disabilities. One organization was the Community Advocacy Centers, or CAC Michigan which has a number of chapters in most Michigan counties. Adults with mental impairment often found enjoyable activities at club meetings. If Mary lived in Alma, she might be a member of the Gratiot County Chapter, and he might be able to talk to her at the next meeting.

Lou called the Gratiot County Chapter office in Ithaca and talked with Gloria Wilber, the director. He learned that Mary was an active member and almost always attended the monthly meetings; the next was in two days. Miss Wilber assured Lou that he would be welcome to attend. And, since Mary was an adult, he didn't need to consult with her legal guardian, Rose, before talking with her.

Lou arrived at the meeting early, greeting each person as he or she entered the gathering place. People were giving hugs and handshakes to one another when Mary walked in. Mary had Downs Syndrome, and, typical of many people with this syndrome, was overweight, yet she was most attractive and wore fashionable clothes, a habit Lou imagined was instilled in her by her mother in her early years and supported by Rose.

Miss Wilber waited till Mary had met all of her friends and then took her aside. "Mary, I'd like you to meet Mr. Searing. Lou, this is Mary McCracken." The two shook hands and exchanged warm smiles.

"Mr. Searing is a detective, and he would like to ask you a few questions. Is that okay with you?"

"Ok."

"Mary, this won't take long," Lou assured her. "I know you are anxious to be with your friends this evening." Mary nodded.

"I want to talk to you because I am helping the sheriff try to solve the murder of Mr. Webberson. Do you know of him?" Lou asked.

"Yes. Rose doesn't like him. The word in the puzzle is underestimate."

"That's right. You know quite a bit."

"Mom said I am psychic."

"Psychic?"

"Yeah, I can predict things. I used to scare my mom with what I knew would happen. She never told anyone. Guess she was trying to protect me. Maybe I upset her?"

"Oh, you're clairvoyant?" Lou asked, then realized that word probably was not in Mary's vocabulary.

"Yeah, that's it! I can't pronounce that, but I know about that."

"Well, that's quite a talent to have."

"Makes me special."

"Yes, it certainly does. Since you know the word, do you know who killed Mr. Webberson?"

"Yes."

"Will you tell me?"

"No."

"Why not? It sure would help us solve this case."

"I won't hurt my friends. So, I won't tell you."

"That's fine, I respect that. But, why would telling me hurt your friends?" Lou asked.

Mary hesitated for several seconds. "I want to go and be with my friends."

"Sure, Mary," Lou replied. "Thanks for talking with me."

Mary rose, shook Lou's hand, and walked out of the room. She stopped short of the door, turned to Lou, and said, "There will be one more murder, and the word on the crossword puzzle will be 'the'."

Lou sat dumbfounded for several seconds, realizing that he had been in the presence of someone who knew, or thought she knew, the answer to the Webberson murder. And, she knew one more murder would be committed. Since she didn't want to hurt her friends, there must be some connection to others at this meeting, or to another set of friends. Maybe she meant the people she had met on lighthouse tours.

Next on Lou's interview list was Rose. She was available, so he went to her home while Mary was at the CAC Chapter meeting. Rose was the perfect example of a Victorian woman; her hair was up in a bun. She was without makeup and she wore a long, flowing dark dress. She seemed quite prim and proper. Her home was decorated in the Victorian style, and for Lou it was like stepping back more than a century in time.

"You are looking into Arthur Webberson's murder, I take it?" Rose asked, after welcoming Lou into her home.

"Yes, the sheriff is short-handed between summer festivals and camps. He asked for my help, and I was happy to oblige."

"You are most kind, but I don't know why you want to talk to me. Certainly you don't think I would have any information to help you."

"You are on my list."

"A list?" Rose asked, confused.

"I create a list of anyone who might have relevant information, and then I talk to each person."

"I see. Well yes, I'll be one of those that doesn't know anything. But, since you are here, go ahead and ask. I've never been interviewed by a detective before. This might prove interesting. Can I offer you something to eat or drink?"

"I've already imposed by interrupting your evening. I'm fine, but you are most kind to offer."

"Okay, question number one. I'm going to love this," Rose said.

"Did you know Mr. Webberson?"

"I knew who he was," Rose answered. "I knew he was very wealthy and was passionate about lighthouses. I know he's always in the way of my purchasing a light. There, that's all I know."

"For not having anything to offer, that's quite a bit."

"Well, that last bit is probably why I am on your list. When I left New York and came back to Michigan to care for Mary, I wanted to buy a lighthouse. I envisioned a gift shop, maybe a bed-and-breakfast. But, Arthur Webberson blocked every turn in the road. Somehow he connived to get first rights to every lighthouse whenever one was for sale."

"That would make the man somewhat unpopular," Lou said.

"Whoever heard of such a thing?" Rose countered, getting more upset as she continued. "Talk about being greedy and controlling! I contacted my senator, my congressman, the president — nobody could or would help. They all said it was legal and was being handled by the appropriate governmental agency."

"I see. So, his demise must have restored your hopes."

"Oh, absolutely! As soon as I heard the news, I began contacting the various holders of deeds, and to be honest, a light already has my name on it. I am so excited!" Her bright smile faltered. "Unfortunately, Mary doesn't share my excitement."

"Mary?"

"Oh, yes, Mary is my sister. I care for her and have done so since our parents died. She is retarded. We both retired from Alma College recently, but Mary still works part-time. I was a music professor, and Mary is in maintenance."

"I see."

"I'm sure Mary is not on your list."

"To be honest, I've already talked to Mary."

"Talked to Mary, without my permission?"

"Mary is an adult, Miss McCracken. She doesn't need your permission to talk to me."

"But courtesy, Mr. Searing. I am her guardian." Rose was becoming agitated. "Certainly she had nothing to say about this. She knows nothing!"

"You were saying that Mary doesn't approve of purchasing this light?"

"No, she likes being around her friends, and I think she fears losing them when we move."

"Seems like a legitimate concern."

"Yes, I suppose, but this is a dream of mine, and she'll adjust."

"I'm sure she will. But, I take it you don't know anything about the murder of Mr. Webberson?"

"Of course not. I didn't like the man, but I am a woman of dignity and compassion. I couldn't set a trap for a mouse, let alone kill someone, or support someone who would."

"Fine, then. Thanks for your time, Miss McCracken."

"I'll show you to the door."

Later that evening, when Mary came home from her club meeting, Rose was quick to ask her about Lou's visit. "Honey, did you talk to a detective tonight?"

"Yes."

"You didn't tell him anything, did you?"

"You mean besides you killed Arthur?" Mary said staring into Rose's eyes.

"Oh, my God. No, honey. Tell me you didn't say that. Tell me you are fooling with me, precious!"

"I told him I was a psychic."

"Oh, Mary, whatever am I going to do with you?" Rose asked.

"You are not taking me to the new lighthouse. I am not going."

"Nonsense, you'll meet wonderful friends, and I can assure you, where we are going, your friends will dress smartly and fashionably."

"The word on the puzzle is 'the'."

Rose, astounded, drew herself up and slapped Mary across the face, then froze as she realized what she had just done.

Mary put her hands to her face, and while sobbing, turned, and walked away.

Rose followed her, remorseful. "I'm so sorry, honey! I'm so sorry! I don't know what came over me. Forgive me, Mary, please forgive me!" Mary continued walking and didn't look back. She had made up her mind that she would never be abused again.

The next morning Lou called the Gratiot County CAC Chapter president, Gloria Wilber.

"Good morning, Lou."

"Good morning. Thanks for making me feel comfortable last evening at the club meeting. I appreciated your help."

"We were happy to have you visit."

"I want to respect Mary's privacy, but she said something that seemed odd, so I wanted to ask you about her remark."

"Mary is odd that way, Lou. She can come up with some very off-the-wall and seemingly believable comments that we later find have no basis in truth. On the other hand, uncanny as it may be seem, she is sometimes quite in tune with reality. What did she say, that she killed someone?"

"No, she said she knew who killed the man, but she wouldn't tell me who that was. This is why I'm calling. She said she didn't want to hurt her 'friends.' I assumed her friends were others in the CAC Chapter, but they could be from somewhere else."

"I suspect most of her friends are here at the club," Gloria explained. "To my knowledge, when she speaks of her friends, she means our members. Well, this might be a fantasy, but there could be some kernel of truth. About a month ago, I wrote to several lighthouses asking if there were any funds set aside to support a visit from a group without resources to pay for a trip. I received four or five responses. Each said no, but they would suggest such a fund to their boards. However, I received a letter from Arthur Webberson, saying he would privately support our trip. He noted in the letter that he has a son with a mental impairment, so helping our group would have special meaning to him.

"He even said that he was willing to conduct the tour personally if we chose the light in Ludington. We accepted his generous contribution and his invitation to visit the Ludington light. Eight of us went on June twenty-seventh, but Mary did not go with us. She and her sister Rose, go on several lighthouse trips a year, so it wasn't a treat for her."

"But where would she get the idea that telling me who killed Arthur would hurt her friends?" Lou asked.

"I think that's just Mary being Mary. She knows Rose is not fond of Mr. Webberson, and she may have told her friends about this. So when he was murdered, she simply jumped to the conclusion that her friends wanted to help her sister by killing the man. Mary lacks an understanding of time, so she could put together that he invited us to a light to meet him and he died. It makes sense to her that her friends killed him to help her and Rose."

"I see. But she knew details of the case. She knew a crossword puzzle was on his body and a word was left unfinished."

"Well, that's explainable, too. On our bulletin board is an article about the murder and, while she doesn't read well, she could pick up information there as well as listen to people in the club talking about it. The group liked Mr. Webberson. He was very kind and compassionate, even bought a lighthouse sweatshirt for each of us. We sent a sympathy card to the family when he died."

"So, you think she is juggling facts she hears and formulating a theory that in her mind makes sense?"

"Exactly."

"Makes sense, I guess. What about her claim that she's clairvoyant?" Lou asked.

"Strange, Lou. Sometimes she does seem to predict an event and we don't know if that's just luck, or something she hears on TV, or if it's a real talent."

"When was she right?"

"Ah, let's see. She told everyone about the devastation of hurricane Katrina."

"Really?"

"Yeah, that's what I mean. She gets them on occasion, but most are shots in the dark, and she doesn't even come close."

"Thanks. You've been most helpful," Lou said.

"Happy to help you, Lou."

In an ironic twist of events, Jenny contacted Lou Searing and asked to speak with him. Lou took the call and agreed to meet her in Williamston, Michigan. Several hours later while sitting near the window of a coffee shop, Lou saw Jenny arrive. As she got out of the car, Lou snapped a photo of her with his digital camera.

After a cordial greeting, and with a latte in front of her, Jenny took a deep breath and began. "I want to explain why I misled you when you interviewed me a while back."

"Fine."

"After we talked, I realized that I was digging a hole for myself, and the more I dug, the deeper I got. You must think I'm as guilty as they come. I guess I'll begin with this, I did not kill Arthur Webberson, and I had nothing to do with the killing of Mr. Webberson. I'll take a lie detector test or whatever it takes to have you accept that I am not involved in this murder. Not only that, I have no information about who might be involved. I'm simply a student doing her practicum at the group home."

"But, you do admit to knowing Ted Webberson, and to telling him you would kill his brother. And that you were in Ludington on the day the murder or disappearance occurred. Correct?"

"Definitely. All that is true, and I have knowledge of poisons, which I obtained doing a term paper for my geriatrics major."

"I'd like you to do me a favor, Jenny."

"Anything, Mr. Searing."

"I'd like to interview you and Ted Webberson together. Are you willing?"

"Yes."

"Okay, that's next, then." The two checked their calendars to find a convenient time.

⬜⬜⬜⬜⬜

Lou arrived at the group home and asked first to speak to Ike, Ted's friend. Ike sat in the empty kitchen, while most of the clients were in the den watching *Let's Make A Deal* or playing games in the dining room.

Lou began, "May I call you, Ike?"

"That's my name, or at least that's my name as far as Ted is concerned."

"Okay, Ike, you're a friend of Mr. Ted Webberson, right?"

"Guess you could say that. We seem to hit it off, and we talk a lot."

"How do you judge his mental faculties?"

"He's all together," Ike said. "Totally together."

"You don't see any delusion, any signs of Alzheimer's, any fantasy, or dementia?"

"I'm no physician, but no, Ted seems intact. Sometimes I think he may pretend to have lost it to get some attention, like from his family, but with me, he never shows anything outside normalcy. But remember, I'm no doctor.

"I like Ted. I can carry on an intelligent conversation with him. We can play chess, do crossword puzzles, debate whether to get out of Iraq or not. Nobody else in this place can do that. If I didn't have Ted here, I'd go nuts in a week."

"Did he kill his brother?"

"Not a chance."

"Did he participate in the killing of his brother? I don't mean physically, but maybe by hiring a hit man, or paying or encouraging someone to act on his behalf?"

"I'm sure he didn't. If you're heading for the Jenny Connection — that's what I call it, the Jenny Connection, that's just a huge joke. She plays along with him, and they both know it."

"Well, please do what you can for Ted and come clean, because this young lady is high on the suspect list."

"I'll talk to him, but Ted's not sorry at all. He couldn't stand his brother — considered him arrogant, selfish, mean-spirited, practically the devil himself."

Jenny arrived at the group home a half hour later. Ted was wheeled into the kitchen where Lou had been talking with Ike.

"Mr. Webberson, my name is Lou Searing. We talked before. If you remember, I'm working with the sheriff in Mason County to solve the murder of your brother, Arthur."

Ted put out his hand, and the two greeted one another.

"I've asked Jenny to meet with us, because the two of you might be able to help."

"I don't want to help," Ted replied, matter of factly.

"That's unfortunate," Lou said, taken aback by Ted's quick and negative response.

"My brother was a good-for-nothing human being. I'm not sorry he's dead, and if I could shake the hand of the person who did him in, I'd do it. I might even buy him a cup of coffee."

"Do you know who killed Arthur?" Lou asked.

"If I did, I wouldn't tell you. I'd do everything I could to keep the guy out of prison."

"Mr. Webberson, did Jenny have anything to do with Arthur's murder?"

"Absolutely not. Jenny is a friend, a wonderful person. She wouldn't kill anybody."

"But you told someone at Arthur's funeral that Jenny killed him."

"I was just trying to be funny. At those morbid places and ceremonies — someone needs to kick up the dust a bit, so I did."

"You sure put Jenny in a difficult spot; you do realize that, don't you?"

"I guess I did. I'm sorry, Jenny. It wasn't funny, and you're the last person I'd want to hurt; you and Ike — you two are the only friends I've got." Jenny bent down and gave Ted a hug.

"Do you have any idea who might have killed your brother?" Lou asked.

"No, and even if I did, I told you, I'd keep it to myself."

"Do you see any kind of setup? After all, an unfinished crossword puzzle was apparently at the scene and you are a fan of doing puzzles." Lou asked.

"Have you any idea of the number of people in this country who do crossword puzzles?" Ted asked, shaking his head. "We number in the millions. Every daily paper worth its salt has a puzzle. The industry is huge. To connect anyone to Arthur's death because he likes to do crossword puzzles is nonsense."

"Good point. Thanks for talking with me, Mr. Webberson."

Jenny moved over and took Ted's hand. "Ted, I am going to have to say goodbye for awhile. My commitment to the home is up, and

I'm taking a full load next semester. I know you appreciate my company, but you knew the practicum was only for a short time."

"Will you stop in and see Ike and me once in a while?" Ted asked solemnly.

"I promise I will, but please don't depend on my being here regularly. OK?"

"Yeah, OK. It's just that you're smart and kind, and I like you."

"I like you, too, Ted."

Tears began to well up in Ted's eyes. Lou felt uncomfortable witnessing the emotional farewell between a bitter old man and a young, compassionate student. It was a nice interaction. Each would miss the other, but Jenny needed space and aught not to be involved with Ted, at least until this case was settled.

When Miss Wilber, the director of the CAC chapter, used the Internet to find a way to contact Arthur Webberson, she wrote A. Webberson in the subject line and hit the "Go" icon. Among the first several items was a Web site for A. Webberson. Miss Wilber thought it was Arthur's Web site, but the name "Andrew" surfaced once she was on the site.

What she found was the Web site of a unique man in London, England, who had Savant Syndrome. Although he was retarded, he could play musical scores after listening to them once, and he seemed to have quite a following. His bio indicated that he was forty years old, had not gone to school, nor had he had any musical training. He had been taken in by an orphanage shortly after birth. His development was that of a three-year-old in terms of his ability to read and communicate. He currently resided in a group home in London, but presented concerts arranged by his agent. Andrew could receive e-mail, but all messages were screened by the attendant at his home.

Miss Wilber sent an e-mail message asking if Andrew was related to the well-known philanthropist, Arthur S. Webberson. A couple of days later she received the following e-mail.

Dear Miss Wilber, Thank you for your kind e-mail. On behalf of Andrew, I will say with a high level of confidence that Andrew does not have a known relative. This does not mean that Andrew is not related to the said Arthur, but such a relationship is unknown to him. Andrew was abandoned by his mother and his orphanage records have been destroyed, making the establishment of relatives nearly impossible. Thank you for your inquiry. On behalf of Andrew Webberson, his attendant/guardian, Henry Postwaite.

Rose was delighted with her recent purchase of a light — it was literally a dream come true. Unfortunately, for every ounce of excitement Rose felt about this new endeavor, Mary felt equally depressed. Her friends at the CAC chapter were her life whenever she wasn't under the thumb and watchful eye of her sister Rose.

Mary believed that in moving to the light, she would become a full-time housekeeper, responsible for cleaning, laundering, and other drudgery. She had had enough of that at Alma College, working on the maintenance staff. Now, her only joy actually was the CAC club. She felt moving to the light would be akin to dying.

The issue came to a head when Rose announced to Mary that they would take a day trip to the light. Mary outright refused to go. Such confrontations had occurred before, and Mary had always yielded to her sister and guardian. But, this time, Mary held her ground. She was dead set against moving.

As the date for their trip to Saugatuck approached, Rose had collected a number of cleaning supplies, tools, and gardening implements. She intended that the two of them should begin the monumental task of fixing up the place and making plans for a cozy cottage.

Mary's only option to be uncooperative was to run away. She had made arrangements with a friend, who could drive, to pick her up during the night and take her to another friend's home. Everything went according to plan and when Rose awoke the next morning, the stark reality of Mary's disappearance was most disturbing.

Mary had left a note: *"I hate light! Will not go! Bye!!"* Not only didn't Rose know where Mary had gone, but her plans for the day had fallen apart, and she felt very disturbed and disappointed. Rose knew that she could go to the light and begin the work herself, but that wasn't her plan.

Rose immediately called the CAC office. The receptionist, who answered the phone, listened to Rose rant and rave, but had no idea of Mary's whereabouts.

Rose was sure Mary couldn't go far because she had no money, no means of travel, and no destination. But as is often the case, as Mary's guardian, Rose didn't appreciate the ingenuity of people with disabilities, and the network of friendships that often exist through advocates and various organizations.

Mary was in sympathetic hands, so she would not be found, at least not soon. Rose hesitated to file a missing persons report; she didn't want the publicity and attention from the authorities that would certainly bring. Any issue related to people with disabilities, especially the possibility of their mistreatment, would be extremely unpopular in the mainstream media as well as in the small community. Rose believed that Mary would eventually come home.

After all, her belongings and her means of survival were under Rose's control.

Rose cancelled her trip to her light; the work would have to wait for another day. She would stay put and wait for a phone call or Mary's approaching footsteps. Rose thought Mary certainly ought to be home before nightfall.

15

Lou wanted to talk to Florence Webberson again. In any non-accidental death, the spouse is suspect until a decision is made that he or she is definitely not involved. Lou usually didn't combine a meal with an interview, but Florence suggested it, so the two met in Chelsea, Michigan, for lunch.

"I knew you would want to talk to me again, Mr. Searing. You have a reputation for being very thorough and I know you've talked to Wally and Virginia."

"That's correct, Mrs. Webberson."

"I am Florence, please."

"Ok, Florence, I do have some questions. So, if I may, I'd like to begin."

"That's fine."

"Did you or Arthur interact with people whom you considered enemies? Did he have habits that were not widely known? Did he have any addictions he tried to keep secret?"

"Chocolate — the man loved chocolate. Is that what you're looking for?" Florence asked.

"Not really. I mean, did he owe money, support a mistress, gamble thousands of dollars — those kinds of behavior."

"I'd like to think I would have known if he had a mistress, and I'm certain he did not."

"As far as you know, his only children are Wally and Victoria?" Lou asked.

"As you know, he was married before, but he never mentioned any children from that marriage, and I know of nothing to indicate that he had children."

"Does the name Alice Livernois mean anything to you?" Lou asked.

"Alice? No, I never heard of Alice Livernois."

"In your mind he was probably perfect, but I often find that people, especially those who meet a tragic end, have unfavorable connections either in business dealings, finances, or relationships. It may be that either you didn't know your husband very well, or he did a great job keeping you out of the loop regarding his personal life."

"Either could be true. We were very independent people. I suppose you can never know your spouse too well. He could have had enemies or dealings with less-than-pleasant people."

"Why did he choose to inform his family of his plans for the distribution of his wealth in such a fashion?" Lou asked.

"Arthur wanted to be loved — and to stir things up."

"I understand the 'to be loved' part, but what do you mean by 'stir things up'?" Lou asked.

"This sounds odd, but Arthur seemed happiest when there was conflict, and when he was at the center of it. Some people watch the soap operas on TV, and some people like to create their own soaps — Arthur liked to create soaps. He reveled in watching conflicts unfold, jealousies flare. He made money. If he became passionate about some endeavor, nutty or intelligent, he let nothing get in his way to make it work."

"You mentioned being loved, and I said I understand that, but maybe I don't. Why would he leave you nothing, give his son more than his daughter, and then leave his brother a pittance in comparison? That doesn't seem a way to inspire love," Lou reasoned.

"Perhaps not. But conflict is a good bet when the daughter sees her mom get nothing, her uncle get a pittance, and her brother get more that she, but wind up with nothing. It happens when the HOMES Lighthouse Association may change its name to the Arthur S. Webberson Lighthouse Association."

"I see. You are not jealous?" Lou asked.

"If truth be known, I have more money than Arthur — I just don't make a deal out of it. My wealth is mostly in oil stocks, and it's nobody's business. I don't need to be loved, and I certainly don't wish to create conflict. So, it was his money and his life, and he could do with it as he wished. I wouldn't have left any of mine to him, should I have passed on before he did."

"Tell me about his brother Ted."

"He's a hoot! As I told you earlier, the man is cuckoo! I mean, you can't help but laugh at him and feel sorry for him in the same breath!"

"Could he have killed Arthur?" Lou asked.

"Anything's possible. Ted certainly had little fondness for Arthur. I don't think Ted has the mental capacity to carry out a murder. Depending on who you talk to, he either can't tell a grape from a pickle, or he should run the country. His mental capacity is anyone's guess. But, if Ted did it, I wouldn't faint in disbelief."

"Florence, you have been most helpful. I am sorry for your loss."

"Thank you. I admit I'm adjusting."

□□□□□

Lou also wanted to speak with Norman Root, the HOMES Association board member who had talked of hastening Arthur's bequest coming to the association. Norman lived in South Haven, so Lou arranged a downtown meeting at a coffee shop. Norman, a tall, thin man about seventy-five, had a full head of white hair. He also sported a moustache and goatee. Lou sensed that either the man had a chip on his shoulder, or he was very nervous. Lou's experience led him to believe the former.

"Mr. Searing?" Norman called out to Lou from a booth in the back.

"Yes. Mr. Root?"

"Correct. Nice to meet you. It's not every day I have the opportunity to speak with a famous detective, let alone a writer. By the way, I have read a couple of your books, and you seem to lead an interesting life."

"I hope you enjoyed the stories."

"Fiction, but each book is based on a previous case, right?" Norman asked.

"Yes, for the most part. I add a few things here and there to make it an interesting read, but the basic crime and the way it was resolved are fairly accurate."

"You probably want to talk to me because Mrs. Windsand opened her big mouth; she'd probably like nothing better than for me to spend some time in the slammer."

"On the contrary, I haven't talked to a Mrs. Windsand. Should I? Might she have something to add to my investigation?" Lou asked.

"Oh, no, I don't think so. I just assumed she told you about me."

"No, but you have me curious: why would she have told me about you? You're involved, perhaps, to make a comment like that."

"Somebody must have told you about me, or why else would we be talking right now?"

"I don't reveal my sources, Mr. Root. However, your name did come to my attention. Now, what can you tell me?"

"I don't know what you want," Norm replied. "You wanted to see me, so I assume you have some questions."

"I do, but I usually give people a chance to make a statement first. That doesn't seem to be the case with you, so I'll ask my questions."

"Fine. Do I need my attorney here?"

"I'm not a police officer, and I'm only asking questions, but if you are more comfortable with an attorney, I wouldn't object, especially if you are sufficiently involved with this crime to warrant one being present."

"I guess I don't really need one then."

"So, Mr. Root, you are a member of the HOMES Lighthouse Association Board of Directors, correct?"

"Yes, for about seven years now."

"And, the board received this letter from Mr. Webberson's attorney," Lou said, putting a copy of the letter in front of Mr. Root.

"No, we were not given a copy of the letter. Our chairperson read the letter."

"Thanks for that clarification. In either event, you were aware of the content of this letter."

"Yes."

"Pretty good news wasn't it?" Lou asked.

"Yes, most definitely. That kind of money would be extremely helpful — would allow us to initiate a number of projects."

"For example?"

"We could purchase lights, restore lights. We could offer additional tours, sponsor seminars, bring nationally-known speakers to address our members. There's no end to how the money could be helpful."

"I can imagine. Did you know Mr. Webberson?" Lou asked.

"No. I met him at a few social occasions, but he wouldn't remember me."

"Did you understand that the gift to the HOMES Association was a bequest only, contingent on Mr. Webberson's death?"

"Yes. I assumed that was the case."

"You didn't expect that it would be portioned out over a period of time, or even donated as a lump sum before his death?"

"No."

"So, you felt that Mr. Webberson's death, if hastened, would be in the best interests of the association?"

"Yes. The sooner he died, the better off we'd be," Norm admitted.

"Also, it would also lessen the chance that he might change his mind for some reason."

"I hadn't thought of that, but, yes."

"You hadn't thought of his changing his mind, but you had thought that an early death would help HOMES?" Lou asked.

"Yes, but that doesn't mean that because I suggested we should get the money sooner, I would kill him."

"Exactly what did you say?"

"I said off-handedly to Mrs. Windsand that I would do what I could to bring the money to us sooner than his natural death. It might have been an inappropriate remark in retrospect, but yes, that's what I said, and why I thought she had turned me in, so to speak."

Lou was busy jotting down notes.

Norman took a deep breath, "Do you mind if I step outside for a smoke? This is a bit nerve-wracking for me."

"Not a problem. Go ahead."

Mr. Root stood up and took a pack of cigarettes out of his shirt pocket and a Bic lighter out of his pants pocket as he headed for the door. He walked out of the World of Coffee Shop, entered his car, and drove away, leaving Lou waiting in the booth.

"Nosy, good-for-nothing guy!" Norman muttered as he drove away. "I don't need someone without authority coming around setting me up with leading questions. I've got better things to do with my time."

About ten minutes later Lou left. Norman, feeling guilty to some degree, felt as if he were in the frying pan and couldn't stand the heat

LeRoy Otterbee, the attorney for Alice Livernois was skeptical about being a detective. It was much more comfortable to stay in Ohio charging by the fraction-of-an-hour for his services than to wander around seeking a man without a clue to his whereabouts. He'd learned early in his career to leave to others the skills he lacked. No one can be a jack-of-all-trades, and yet, here he was accepting a gig to try and find someone.

The easiest thing to do was hire the work out. He thought a thirty-percent payout was fair. If a true detective found Alice Livernois' father, he would find three hundred thousand dollars in his bank account, and in this day and age, that was pretty good money for tracking someone down.

⬜⬜⬜⬜⬜

Again, Lou called Gloria Wilber at the Gratiot County CAC. "You have been most helpful, so I find myself coming back with more questions."

"Glad to help if I can," Gloria replied.

"When we talked earlier, you told me that when Mr. Webberson was helpful to you when you contacted him for support. He said he had a son who was mentally-impaired. Right?"

"That's correct."

"Do you know this son's name or where he might be? Is he living, or has he passed away?"

"I really don't know, but I do have an idea. It might be a good lead or it may be worthless, but I'll leave that up to you. When I went on the Internet to locate information about Arthur Webberson, I typed 'A. Webberson' into the search engine. I opened the first site, thinking it was Arthur's, but it was for an Andrew Webberson, who has a mental impairment, and who lives in England. His bio says — well you can read it for yourself — he has Savant Syndrome and was placed in an orphanage at birth, so he doesn't know his parents. And he doesn't respond to e-mail, so you need to go through an attendant or guardian."

"Thank you very much. I'll visit the site and see if anything else is helpful."

"Glad I could help, Mr. Searing."

"One more thing, please, Gloria. When you saw Mr. Webberson at the Big Sable Light, did he say anything about this son, or for that matter, give you any indication he expected to die soon?"

"No, nothing was said about a son, and he seemed just fine when we visited with him. He was very cordial, made us feel at ease and thanked us for coming."

"Did he give you a business card, or send you a letter on letterhead?"

"Yes, as a matter of fact, he gave me a business card, but no letter. Why?"

"The name on the card. What is it?" Lou asked.

"Arthur S. Webberson."

"No Junior or Esquire, or degrees after his name?" Lou asked. "The middle name isn't spelled out?"

"No, just his name, Arthur S. Webberson."

Rose was becoming quite concerned; it had been more than forty-eight hours since Mary had left, or perhaps had been abducted. She had called all of Mary's friends, and not one had any idea where Mary was, or where she might be.

One of the friends Rose called, Sherry Bate, had lied, because she was sheltering Mary. Hal and Sherry Bate had worked with her on the maintenance staff at Alma College, and they understood her far better than Rose. They knew the difficulties involved in a disability, and they understood the importance of close friendships for everyone.

On several occasions at work, Mary had ranted and raved about her sister being demanding and treating her poorly. Sherry and Hal didn't know how accurate Mary's words were, but if half of what she said were true, the Bates sympathized with Mary's situation. When Mary told them that Rose had purchased a light and she would have to move and work all the time, the couple offered to have her come and live with them. They had an extra bedroom and lived within walking distance of the college. Mary could be fairly independent, enjoy her friends, and be much happier than if she were expected to work for her sister's dream of owning a light.

Sooner or later Rose would have to go to the police and file a missing person report. After all, if Mary was in danger, Rose's not informing the authorities would be a form of abuse. That could be as much trouble to her as filing a report and apologizing if Mary was found healthy.

This was very disturbing to Rose. For years she had battled Arthur Webberson, who firmly held control of lighthouses around Michigan. Now, she was battling her sister who wanted nothing to do with a move and who would not cooperate to make Rose's dream come true. One thing was clear: Rose was leaving Alma, and she would keep the light, making it into a bed-and-breakfast, with or without Mary. The dilemma was that she had promised her parents before they died that she would care for Mary. They had not wanted Mary to go into a home or some unfriendly place that would make her unhappy. Rose decided not to call the police, and the stalemate entered its third day.

16

Lou contacted his travel agent to set up a trip to London, planning a couple of work days there and maybe one more for sight-seeing. He told the agent that he planned to be in the city of London proper. He didn't want to rent a car, not trusting his capability of driving on the "wrong" side of the road. Getting used to this in London, instead of in a rural community, made him quite anxious.

Lou and Carol were to fly from Grand Rapids to Chicago on July 25, and then catch a direct flight to London. They would stay at the River Thames Hotel. The agent also suggested shows currently playing in the London Theater District, which would be a special treat.

Lou had not cleared this with Carol, wanting to surprise her. He hoped this would be acceptable; he wouldn't like it if Carol pulled this on him, but Carol was a totally different person than Lou in many ways. He was betting she'd say, "Let's go!" and be ready in hours.

Rose couldn't wait any longer for Mary to return. Life was for living and she wanted to get to her light. First she unpacked a sign she'd had made in anticipation of someday owning a light and having a bed and breakfast. Quite attractive in design, the words burned into the wooden sign read: "RoseMary's Baby." She considered it a unique name for a light, or for a B and B for that matter. She didn't realize that, from a marketing standpoint, "Rosemary's Baby" might conjure up frightening images, and the relatively cheerful sign might scare people away rather than invite them to stay the night.

It was late afternoon by the time Rose arrived in Saugatuck. She was tired, but she didn't hesitate to drive to her light to realize her dream, parking in the lot reserved for visitors. Admiring her new possession, she snapped pictures from all angles and distances. She would start a scrapbook and fill it with memories of her light.

Using the key provided to her by the authority that allowed her to purchase the light, she walked in and was pleasantly surprised by how attractive the interior was and how clean the place appeared to be. Evidently a cleaning crew had been there to ready the property for its new owner. She slowly walked through the light, exploring every corner, deciding which would be her bedroom, and where Mary would stay.

Rose liked the décor in the living room. She noticed a small but appropriate collection of magazines: *The Great Lakes Holiday, Boating for Fun, The Lights Around the World.* Lying on top of them was a crossword puzzle magazine. In and of itself, that was fine; but when she opened it, she found the first puzzle was finished, and the second puzzle was half-completed, with a word that was partially filled in. She felt a wave of adrenaline, became lightheaded, and suddenly needed to sit down. Once she collected herself, she was able to continue her work. She destroyed the crossword puzzle before leaving for home several hours later.

Gloria Wilber of the CAC received an e-mail from Henry Postwaite, the attendant/guardian for Andrew Webberson.

Dear Miss Wilber, You may recall writing to ask if Andrew was related to Arthur S. Webberson. I indicated to you that I did not know, but doubted the probability because we have never been able to identify Andrew's parents. However, upon further thought, it seems the Webberson you are looking for might be Andrew's father. Webberson is not a common name, and I should think that Andrew's father would be around sixty. Andrew is quite tall and thin and a bit eccentric, apart from his unique piano skills. Andrew shows signs of becoming bald. I mention these physical attributes because, genetics being what they are, when you find the gentleman you are seeking, his physical characteristics may be similar to Andrew's. Please let me know if you manage to locate Mr. Arthur S. Webberson and whether his characteristics are similar to Andrew's.

Gloria replied to the e-mail message. Her response was short, and a lie.

I was able to contact Mr. Arthur S. Webberson and have met with him. Andrew's physical attributes do not bear any resemblance to Arthur's.

Rose became more concerned about Mary. She wanted to care for Mary, but her absence from home might signal a desire for independence. Maybe Mary could blend into society without Rose's constant supervision. Since Rose knew the calendar of meetings for the CAC Chapter, she drove to the next meeting and watched from a distance to see if Mary arrived. She did, with friends, and happily entered the building. Now Rose knew that Mary was okay, and in her relief, she thought perhaps all was happening for the best.

The next morning, Rose called the CAC and left a message for Mary and the CAC leadership detailing how she could be reached in case contact was needed. She would sell her home in Alma and move to the light. Following the phone call, Rose went to the cemetery where her parents were buried and had a heart-to-heart talk with them. She had promised to take care of Mary, but Mary apparently preferred to live on her own. If Rose was letting her parents down, she was sorry, but she had chosen to live a new life also. Rose drove home from the cemetery content that all would be well.

Mr. Otterbee, the attorney for Alice Livernois contracted the search for Arthur Webberson to a computer-literate college student named Joseph Day. Joseph took the copy of Alice's birth certificate and the marriage license issued to Arthur Dickenson and started his search. When he found no death certificate for an Arthur Dickenson, age 65, born in Struthers, Ohio, on October 9, 1941, he decided to forget the name Dickenson, and concentrate on the wife's maiden name, Abigail Wallace. And, at the same time, Joseph hoped to locate the minister who married them, a Reverend William Peach, if he was still living.

He found a newspaper account corresponding to the date and location of the wedding in the archives of a newspaper on the Internet. He noted that the maid of honor was Shirley Straastma, and the best man was John Halverson.

Joseph found the obituary of Abigail Wallace Dickenson who Alice Livernois told her attorney had died on December 16, 1992 in Lima. He easily found her obituary. This led to a dead end because Abigail's only survivors were her son and daughter and he already had that information. But, he noticed that the funeral was at St. Thomas Catholic Church in Lima, and he knew that church records often contained more information; if there were church directories, he might even find a picture of the couple.

Joseph made arrangements with the secretary of St. Thomas to search the records for anything regarding an Arthur Dickenson or an Abigail Wallace Dickenson, as well as a possible photo. The church secretary was not very cooperative, none too pleased to provide information to someone outside the Dickenson family, but a promised donation to the church seemed to ease her apprehension.

According to the relevant marriage document, the last names of Arthur and Abigail were the same. That's odd, Joseph thought. It could be the truth, or the recorder simply may have made a mistake and written Dickenson for both the bride and groom. There was no photo of the couple in the old church directories.

Lou was becoming obsessed with the crossword puzzles on the victims' bodies; there had to be a connection between them. He put the four puzzles side-by-side in the order of the murders. The three words that were not filled in were "greed," "never," "underestimate," and "power." The missing letters were G, N, E, V, E and R. And, if this indicated a serial killer, which Lou considered nearly impossible, since the murders at the light occurred more than eighty years apart, how could anyone know of the details of a murder in 1925, much less want to copy the behavior of a murderer long since deceased?

There was no question that the murderer was playing a game, so Lou called his seven-year-old grandson in Grand Rapids, Jackson Searing, who was a detective wannabe. He might be able to come up with something.

"Hi, Grandpa."

"Hi, Jackson. Are you willing to help me solve a mystery, young man?"

"Cool! Yeah!"

"Well, I'd like you to try to find a pattern or a connection between these words or figure out what they have in common."

"Have in common? Like kinda the same?" Jackson asked.

"Yes. I think there is a clue in these words, but I can't seem to put my finger on it."

"Clue, like a name or something?"

"Yeah, maybe. You know what a crossword puzzle is, right?"

"Yeah."

"Okay, the words I'm going to give you are the answers to four different clues in a crossword puzzle; and some letters were missing in each word. Maybe the secret is in the missing letters."

"I need to get paper and a pencil. Can you talk to Daddy?"

"Sure." Lou and Carol's son, Scott got on the line.

"Sounds like you're looking to young Sherlock for some free advice," Scott said.

"Well, he's sharp enough that he may figure something out. Perhaps the words aren't in his vocabulary, so you may need to work with him."

"Sure. What's this all about?" Scott asked.

"I'm not telling him, but a crossword puzzle has been found on or near each victim in a case I am investigating. In each puzzle, a word is incomplete, so I think the murderer is playing cat-and-mouse with the authorities. There has to be some connection, and I thought Jackson might see something that I can't."

"Here he is, ready to go. You might want to tell me the words and the missing letters, so we'll be sure he gets them right. And, are you giving him the words in the order they were found?"

"Yes. The words are 'greed,' 'never,' 'underestimate,' and 'power'; the missing letters are G, N, E, V, E, and R."

"Ok, here's Jackson."

"Ok, I'm ready, Grandpa."

"I'll give you the words and then you can underline the missing letters, OK, Jackson?"

"Yup, go ahead." Lou repeated the information, and Jackson read them back. So, he now had everything that Lou had.

"Good luck, young Sherlock."

"It would be really neat if I could solve this, Grandpa."

"Well, you have as good a chance as I have. You might make sense of it all. Have fun."

"Ok. Bye."

Jackson got right to work. He scrambled all the letters and, with Scott's help, tried to make words using all the letters his Grandpa had given him. His attention span was fairly long, but after fifteen minutes or so, he decided that a video game was much better enter-tainment for a while.

Scott, on the other hand, continued to try to figure out the mystery. He took each word apart by syllable and tried to make words out of the syllables. He tried to spell something out of the first letters, then the second letters, and so forth. Nothing seemed to make any sense. He saw the obvious 'REVENGE' but he needed one more E.

Wally and Bea were obvious suspects, deprived of millions of dollars when they had planned on their inheritance supporting them for the rest of their lives. Neither had any significant talent or skill. Having a good time was their major in college, but after graduation, life caught up with them, and wild college behavior quickly became a thing of the past.

Bea and Wally each suspected the other in the death of Arthur. They were not together at the time of the murder, and neither could trust the other since each had been caught red-handed telling "white lies." The lies were minor infractions, but the damage showed in their mutual lack of trust. There had been little love in their relationship, and being cut out of the will brought constant stress and conflict.

Neither directly accused the other of murder, but there was a constant undercurrent of suspicion. Bea loved crossword puzzles, and Wally thought she could be the culprit in a copy-cat murder. However, he was absolutely certain that Bea was not involved in the murder of the woman on the catwalk in Manistee.

Bea knew Wally had a mean streak in him; he had shown that on more than one occasion. She, more than anyone, knew how furious Wally was to be left out of his father's will. And though Wally's attorney had advised him that his father must live for Wally to have any chance at an inheritance, Bea believed his anger probably took precedence over legal advice. Besides, she figured that Wally would file suit, tying up the estate for most of his adult life. Supporting Bea's thoughts was a comment Wally had made to a friend, "By golly, if I don't get that money, nobody will, least of all a bunch of lighthouse nuts!"

17

JULY 22

In Charlevoix, the Greenville school group had reservations at a public campground. Some of the students pitched a tent while others went exploring, looking for the beach or an ice cream store. After they were all comfortable with their surroundings, Andrew and William went to the library with Jack who had driven his own car to Charlevoix.

The librarian knew a lighthouse historian, who as luck would have it, was in the library when Andrew and William stopped in. "Her name is Mrs. Autumn Angers, and she's sitting over there in the light brown jacket."

Andrew and William approached the elderly woman. "Excuse me, Mrs. Angers. May we talk with you?" Andrew asked.

"You already are, so continue. But first, please tell me who you are?"

"I'm Andrew Hinman and this is William Jackson," Andrew began. "We're researching the 1925 murder at the Squaw Island Lighthouse. The librarian said you know lots about lighthouses in the Great Lakes," Andrew began.

"Yes, I guess I do."

"Does that include the lighthouse on Squaw Island?"

"Yes. I don't think there is another person living who knows more than I do."

"Do you know of any published history of the lighthouse?"

"Yes, but why are you interested?" Mrs. Angers asked.

"It's for a class project. We go to high school in Greenville, and about twenty of us are here to find out as much as we can about the lighthouse out there."

"I see. Have you ever been in that lighthouse?"

"No. And our teacher, Mrs. Bell, wasn't able to get permission," William said, with a look of disappointment.

"That I can fix, because I have the key. Have your teacher contact me, and I'll send it to her. OK?"

"Fantastic!! Thanks a lot!" William and Andrew said in unison, imagining they had really struck gold.

"I've written a book, or probably I should say, a booklet entitled, *The Squaw Island Light: Separating Fact from Fiction.*"

"Perfect. Can we get a copy?" Andrew asked.

"I don't have any copies to loan you, but I suspect our librarian can find a copy in the stacks."

"Do you discuss the 1925 murder of Mr. Edwards?" William asked.

"Yes. And I regret what happened to me after I got too close to the scene and learned things that no one was meant to know."

"'Happened to you'?" Andrew questioned.

"I'd rather not talk about it, but let's just say some things are meant to remain mysteries, and this may one of them."

"I see."

"Please tell me why you are so interested in the murder of Mr. Edwards."

William and Andrew looked at one another questioningly. "I guess I can share our project," Andrew began. "Do you know Lou Searing?"

"Lou Searing, the detective?" Autumn asked.

Both boys nodded.

"Oh, my yes, he is a favorite of mine. I've never met him, so I guess I shouldn't say I know him, but I feel like I know him from reading his books. He solves some humdingers, doesn't he?"

"He sure does. He came to our class a year ago and talked about his novels. We enjoyed his talk, and he gave each of us an autographed book. After the murder of Mr. Webberson our teacher, Mrs. Bell asked him if we would like us to help him solve it. He agreed."

"He wouldn't have agreed unless he knew you kids were responsible."

"I suppose he's taking a risk," Andrew replied. "But, Mrs. Bell has made it very clear that our responsibility is to handle this well."

"We were saying on the way up here that, if we can't give him some good leads, we'll feel like we let him down," William added.

"Well, like I've always said, there's nothing like reality to do the teaching," Mrs. Angers said, smiling.

"Thanks for your help. We'll ask to check out your booklet," Andrew said.

"Can we ask you questions if we uncover something?" William asked.

"Certainly. I'm here in the library most every day. It's comfortable, and more sociable than in my small apartment."

"Thanks again."

"Good luck." As they began to leave, she got their attention and motioned them back. "Might you two be able to get me an autographed copy of Mr. Searing's book about this Webberson murder once it's published? I can't think of anything that would make me happier."

"I imagine so," William said. "He is a nice guy. He may come up and give you a copy himself. That's the kind of guy he is, very low-key and friendly."

"That would be wonderful."

"Before we go find your book, one more question, please," Andrew said.

"Yes?"

"Are the relatives of the killer still alive, and do you know who they are?"

"The answer to both of your questions is, yes, but that's all you will hear from me. Read my story and enjoy your work with Mr. Searing. But I've one bit of advice so you don't encounter the difficulty I had. Do not disturb anything in the light. Do not move any furniture, or even move a curtain."

"Because?" Andrew asked.

Mrs. Angers grew a little agitated. "Please listen to me, do not move anything when you are in the light. When you and your friends are ready to go, I will give your teacher the key and repeat this important warning."

"Yes, ma'am, we understand," William replied, respectfully.

The boys checked out the booklet, flipping a coin to see who got to read it first. The coin landed on the back of William's hand. "Tails!" Andrew would read first.

The murder of Mr. Edwards occurred the evening of August 4, 1925 around eleven o'clock. According to Mrs. Edwards, the family was asleep when she was awakened by an intruder. When Mrs. Edwards got up and lit a candle she saw on the bedroom wall the shadow of a person who appeared to be wearing a wide-brimmed hat. Ironically, she said the figure reminded her of a pirate with his face covered with a black mask. She recalled seeing the shadow move toward her husband. Mr. Edwards awoke just as a sword entered his throat and pushed up into his brain. He made a gurgling sound and went limp. Mrs. Edwards was not harmed physically, but she was in shock. She heard the intruder say, "He dies because he saw me take the gold," but she has no memory of anything after hearing the voice except the terrifying look on her husband's face, seen in the light of the flickering candle.

The boys very quickly identified the three aspects of any crime: the victim, Mr. Edwards; a weapon, the sword; and a motive, for Mr. Edwards had witnessed a crime in progress. The murderer, a man dressed in black, looking like a pirate, and admitted the motive for his crime.

No weapon was ever found in or around the light, and no gold was ever reported either stolen or found. No blood was found on the bedding or in any part of the bedroom of the lighthouse. And, according to the medical report, there was no wound on Mr. Edwards' body. In fact, the cause of death on the death certificate was listed as a heart attack.

There remains the question whether a murder actually occurred. Perhaps Mrs. Edwards had a dream, or maybe she killed her husband and made up the story to confuse the authorities. The sheriff's report reads, 'The door to the light was forced open, because the handle was torn from the frame. There were muddy footprints on the floor in the entry, though it had not rained for three days. The most obvious suspect is the son, Joseph. It was well-known that Joe did not get along with his father. Most likely Mrs. Edwards did see the shadow of someone who may have been brandishing a sword, but more likely Mr. Edwards actually had a heart attack, and Mrs. Edwards, in her delirium, believed she saw the weapon plunge into her husband's throat and skull. I recommend to the constable that no charges be filed, as I am unable to either find witness or weapon, and there are great inconsistencies between evidence I collected and the statement from Mrs. Edwards. Case closed.'

"Weird!" Andrew exclaimed.

While the students in Charlevoix contacted interesting people and began learning about the murder of the light keeper, Lou was pursuing a discovery of his own. It appeared that the Great Lakes had provided their own high-seas dramas. Lou was coming to the realization that bands of thieves, or pirates, if you will, worked not only the coastal areas of the oceans, but also the shores of the Great Lakes, the largest aggregation of inland lakes in the world.

Lou reasoned that where there were pirates, there would be bounty, a good incentive to rob and plunder. The ships plying the Great Lakes likely carried cargo other than ore and lumber, sometimes cargos of great value, and taking them from a Great Lakes shipping vessel might have been surprisingly easy.

Perhaps the major deterrents to crime were the watchful eyes of the lightkeepers. They could intercept distress calls, and sometimes even observe the raid, depending on shore and lake conditions.

While Andrew and William pored over the booklet describing the murder of Mr. Edwards, the other students planned a trip to the lighthouse to survey the area, take photos, and determine the layout of the structure, inside and out. At dinner, the students, Mrs. Bell, and Ms. Scheiern talked about what they had learned and formulated plans for the next day.

"I'd like to say something," Andrew began. "While William and I were talking with Mrs. Angers, the town historian and the author of the booklet we brought back from the library, she said she had a key to the light, which she'd lend to you, Mrs. Bell. We could go inside, but she cautioned us not to move anything. She made that point a couple of times."

"Why the special caution?" Ms. Scheiern asked.

"She said she doesn't want any of us to have experiences like she had when she was looking into the murder."

"What's that supposed to mean?" Mrs. Bell asked.

"She wouldn't say; she just kept repeating that we must not move anything, not even a drape. Right, William?"

"That's what she said."

"Boy, now you really have me curious," said James Hopkins. "I am not usually a daredevil, but I'd sure like to know what happens if something is moved."

"Well, we are not going to find out," Mrs. Bell said with emphasis. "And to simplify matters, the only people going into the light are Ms. Scheiern or me, and…"

"No, thank you!" Ms. Scheiern exclaimed. "I'll stay back, perfectly content to hear about your adventure when you return."

"Ok, then I'll go, and the five students chosen to go to the Island will draw straws to see who goes into the lighthouse."

Kim Barber spoke up, "You mean, you four can draw straws. Entering a ghostly lighthouse isn't my idea of fun or adventure."

Mrs. Bell said calmly, "Well, I'm going in with someone, whether one of the Hardy Boys or Nancy Drew, it matters not to me. Just find a way to choose. But, when you choose, I don't want anyone who is clumsy, because we're not going to move a thing. Except to open the door to go in and close it when we leave, we won't touch anything!"

"Let's decide this now," Kyle Campbell said. "Anyone else want out, or are we choosing from the four of us?"

"I'm out," Stephanie Stump replied. "Call me chicken, but I'm not taking a chance. Besides, some dead guy was in there, and that gives me the creeps."

"Ok, it's between Justin Aylesworth, Gabe Bruning, and me," Kyle said. "What's fair?"

"I suggest we each tell why we should be the one to go in and when the three of us are finished, each of us will have one vote," Gabe suggested. "Whoever gets the most votes, goes. Fair?"

"Sure," Justin said. "I'll go first."

"I want to go in because when Mr. Searing investigates a crime, he goes right to the center of the case. If he were here, he'd go into the light, right, Mr. Kelly?" Jack nodded. "Since we're working for him, in a sense, I want to be one who goes in."

Kyle spoke next. "I'm curious. I'm the bear who goes over the mountain to see what he can see. There might be something important in that light, and nothing would please me more than to see it and record it. I'm itching to go in!"

Gabe was the final speaker. "I don't feel as strongly as Justin and Kyle, but I would like to go in representing all the people who donated to our fund-raisers. Those folks trusted us to make this trip worthwhile, to help solve the murder of Mr. Webberson. So, I won't be hurt or disappointed if I don't set foot inside the light, but I really would like to see it for myself."

Mrs. Bell gave everyone a small piece of paper. Each was to write the first name of the person they wanted to enter the lighthouse, and yes, it was permissible to vote for one's self.

Ms. Scheiern counted the votes and announced the winner. "The person going into the light with Mrs. Bell is Gabe Bruning. Congratulations, Gabe."

Gabe gave each student a high-five, thanked everyone, and promised to be observant. "I can't promise I won't accidentally move something, but if I do, and the lady is right, then I hope whatever happens only happens to me."

That evening everyone had s'mores around a campfire and took turns telling ghost stories. Some of the stories were pretty good.

Jack had made arrangements with John Tromp to transport Mrs. Bell, five students and himself to Squaw Island on July 23. John had studied his charts and researched the trip so it wouldn't offer any surprises. The weather was perfect, which was what John, his son and first mate, Jonathan, and their toy fox terrier, Cody had hoped for.

Departure was to be at ten o'clock from an Amoco fueling station beside the public marina in downtown Charlevoix. Jack and Mrs. Bell made sure the five students had a good breakfast and then purchased some box lunches. It was going to be a hot, clear day, so suntan lotion, shirts, and hats were required.

The yacht, christened the *Admiralty,* left the dock and pulled into the line awaiting the half-hourly drawbridge opening. Once past the bridge, the boat would move through the channel and out past the lighthouse into Lake Michigan. The *Admiralty,* a Carver Aft Cabin craft was about thirty-five foot long, with three tiers: on top was the bridge; three steps down was the aft deck, with chairs and tables; and the final three steps led down to the salon and galley. The boat was plenty big for the passengers making the trip to Squaw Island. The students expressed the feeling they had died and gone to heaven, as none of them had ever been on a yacht like this before.

The trip would take about two hours, and with perfect weather, John and Jonathan didn't expect any problems. The students, curious about the radio system, enjoyed John's conversation with some salmon fishermen. Jonathan took the controls while John gave his passengers a quick tour of the boat, pointing out safety features and making sure that everyone felt at home.

The trip over proved uneventful. There was no dock at Squaw Island, so John needed to drop anchor off the island. There wasn't much wind, but to be safe, he dropped the anchor on the east or leeward side, for the wind direction was from the west. Jonathan took people to shore in the dinghy. While he probably could have gotten them all to Squaw Island in two trips, he took three to be safe.

John and Jonathan stayed with the boat while Jack, Mrs. Bell, and the students approached the lighthouse with caution. There was nobody on the island or for miles around, but they looked left and right and behind them as they walked toward the light, as if expecting someone or something to suddenly appear.

Each student had responsibilities. Kyle, the official photographer, took many digital photos all around the lighthouse. He later gave his camera to Gabe with specific instructions to photograph anything interesting inside.

Stephanie and Justin carried metal detectors and spent their time combing the beach and wild area around the lighthouse. Each listened carefully to the ticking of the search coil unit, fantasizing about finding some clue that would help solve the murder.

The fifth student, Kim, was to record any and all experiences of the investigation team. She chronicled all the activity — who found what, and also recorded students' ideas, observations, and theories.

Jack performed an important function, for in reality, he was acting as Lou in absentia. He would offer advice if asked, but for the most part, this trip belonged to the students. Jack did want to go into the lighthouse, but he chose not to do so, because he trusted the observations of Gabe and Mrs. Bell.

Mrs. Bell had gotten the key from Mrs. Anger the night before in Charlevoix. She and Gabe were a bit anxious, but determined. The others watched intently as the explorers approached the structure. After all, to anyone's knowledge, no one had set foot in the lighthouse in decades.

With great trepidation, Mrs. Bell turned the key in the lock and, with a little help from Gabe, pushed open the heavy door. It was partially wedged after years of not swinging on the hinges and withstanding all sorts of weather.

Entering the light, Mrs. Bell and Gabe noticed first the obvious odor of dead animals. Muffled sounds alerted them to scurrying mice, and perhaps an owl or other birds who had found a way inside the light. Once the noises were identified, they recognized layers of dust, dirt, and sand. Each step, or the slightest movement of air, caused dust to dance in the rays of sunlight coming through the doorway.

The furniture was musty and dirty. Several pictures hung on the wall, draped with cobwebs and none of them hung squarely. In the dining area, the armoire held dishes and a dusty moth-eaten cloth covered a table. The kitchen looked as if the cook had walked out after a meal and never returned. Pots and pans were scattered around the floor. Some home-canned peaches in the pantry looked like specimens in a high school biology lab. The bedrooms looked undisturbed. Surprisingly, each bed was made, and a Bible rested on a table next to the master bed. After a thorough cleaning, the place wouldn't look bad, but on this hot July afternoon, it was a mess. Mrs. Bell could only imagine what was drifting into her lungs with each breath.

Mrs. Bell had told Gabe earlier that she had changed her mind about not moving anything. She had decided to disregard Mrs. Anger's warning. They came this far to search, which meant opening drawers and moving things around. Gabe found some reassurance in Mrs. Bell's comment: "After all, Mrs. Angers is still alive so whatever she experienced didn't kill her."

Whatever Mrs. Bell and Gabe hoped to find, they encountered nothing relating to a murder. They found only an old and very dirty lighthouse that had been uninhabited for over eighty years. Since the lighthouse beacon was accessible without going through the home, the two reasoned that while service to the light continued, no one was willing to live in the keepers' quarters after the murder.

There was some evidence of breaking into the home. No doubt young people had damaged the place for fun. But, windows were tightly boarded up and doors securely locked so nobody was able to actually enter the living spaces.

The remainder of the team, left behind in Charlevoix, waited anxiously for a report. Their plan for their day was to visit some lighthouses around Traverse City. Ms. Scheiern called Mrs. Bell every couple of hours to find out how the voyage was going and to report on their shore-side goings on.

In mid-afternoon, while Gabe and Mrs. Bell were in the decrepit lighthouse on Squaw Island, a strange thing happened at the campsite outside of Charlevoix. Kyle Campbell came running from the RV:

"Listen to this! I found a note on the table in the RV: *'The world as you know it is coming to an end. Read about it in the word of God'!*"

"What's that supposed to mean?" Nicole asked.

"Who wrote it? Where did you find it?" Steven wanted to know.

"How would I know who wrote it? It was on the table in the motor home," Kyle replied.

"Okay, game's over, guys," Ms. Scheiern said, with a smile. "Who's playing the joke here? I know things have gotten a little slow and boring, and we haven't exactly helped Mr. Searing yet, but let's not get each other spooked. Fess up. No consequences — just tell us who wrote it." Silently, each one looked at the others.

"I don't think it came from any of us," Nicole said.

"Was the RV locked while we were away?" Ms. Scheiern asked.

"You have the only key, and we've seen you lock it before we go anywhere," Michelle answered.

"Because the motor home belongs to the principal, I have been very careful about making sure it's safe while we're away from it."

"Let's assume that someone else wrote the note," Stephanie said. "I think we should focus on what the note means rather than figuring out who wrote it and put it in the RV."

"This is very spooky," James said.

"I didn't come up here for this," Jordan replied, shivering and looking pale. "Adventure, yes. Happenings from the great beyond, no. Maybe aliens are here to shake us up."

"Hey, hey, listen up!" Ms. Scheiern said firmly. "We're not encountering aliens here, so don't get carried away. I'm sure there's a good explanation for what's happened; we just haven't figured it out yet."

"Let's analyze this," Stephanie suggested once again. "'The world as you know it is coming to an end. Read about it in the word of God'."

"The word of God is the Bible, right?" Ryan said.

"Yes, I guess it is, for Christians anyway, assuming we are talking about the New Testament," Stephanie answered.

"And, the world coming to an end is in the book of Revelation, right?" Ryan asked.

"So, is that the clue? Read the book of Revelation?" Kyle asked.

"I guess so. I don't know what else it could mean," Ms. Scheiern reasoned.

"Does anyone have a Bible?" Rebecca asked.

"I have one in my duffel bag," Kim said. "It's in the tent."

Soon Kim appeared and said, "This is weird, guys; my Bible isn't in my bag."

Kim's cell phone rang. Before answering she said, "This better be a real person, or I am going to faint! Hello."

"Believe me, Mom; I am so glad to hear your voice."

Kim listened to her mother. "That's nice to hear. Anyway, I am only calling to tell you that you forgot your Bible. I found it on your bed."

"Oh, good," Kim said. "We've been so busy up here, I just haven't felt the urge to read it. Thanks for calling, Mom."

"How is everything going? Having fun?"

"Well, I'm not sure I would call it fun. Maybe 'interesting' would be the word right now. I'll tell you and Dad all about it when I get home. Bye, Mom."

Kim turned to her classmates. "That was my mom. I left my Bible at home."

"That takes care of that mystery. The ghost wasn't responsible for our little drama," Ms. Scheiern said. "But, we still don't have an explanation for the note. There's still time for someone to come clean. The fun is over." Nobody spoke.

The group of explorers nearly finished with their work on Squaw Island, had signaled for the dinghy to return to the *Admiralty* when Mrs. Bell's cell phone rang. It was Ms. Scheiern.

"Yes," Mrs. Bell said. "We're about to head back to the mainland."

"Well, don't move so fast," Ms. Scheiern replied. "We've had a strange occurrence over here at the campsite. You may not want to hurry home."

"What's that?"

"Any chance you found a Bible in that light?"

"There was one in the bedroom. Yeah."

"Well, you want to turn to book of Revelation and see if you notice anything."

"Okay, but why?"

"We found a strange note in the motor home mentioning the end of the world and the word of God, and the only thing we can make of the message is the book of Revelation. If there is a Bible in the Squaw Island Light, there could be a connection."

"Perfect timing for your call. Another half hour, and we would have been on the boat back to Charlevoix. I'll go back to the light and see if that Bible has anything interesting. Stay tuned."

Mrs. Bell put the phone in her pocket and turned to Gabe. "We're going back into the light to check something in that Bible in the bedroom."

Stephanie and Justin once again went over the beach between the light and the shore with their metal detectors, covering nearly every inch, like sweeping a mine field. In only an hour they had found a few coins, a class ring, a couple of nails, and a key.

"Could the key we found be related to the case?" Justin asked.

"I don't think so," Mrs. Bell replied. "The teeth aren't the same as the key to the lighthouse."

"That makes sense, but remember Mr. Searing's comment to us that in investigating crime, you can't rely on obvious conclusions with what you find?" Stephanie said.

"That's a good point, but a key needs a lock, or it's just a key."

"But, where there's smoke, there's probably fire," Gabe said.

"Meaning?"

"Meaning where we found the key, we might find the lock."

"Right, but you didn't find a lock."

"But the detector can only sense objects to about three inches into the sand."

"Where are you going with this, Justin?" Mrs. Bell asked.

"I think that this key didn't just slip out of someone's pocket or purse within the last eighty years. This key could match a lock buried in the area where I found the key."

"Highly unlikely," Mrs. Bell responded.

"Yes, but Mr. Searing would dig to rule out the connection," Justin said.

"I think you're right. Do you recall where you found the key?"

"Every find is marked in our log book."

"Okay, take a shovel, and you can dig till it is time to go. Good luck!"

Mrs. Bell and Gabe walked back to the light and opened the door. Gabe went straight to the bedroom where he had seen the Bible. When he opened the volume to find the book of Revelation, he noticed a small corner of an envelope sticking out of the pages further back. Marking the first page of the book of Revelation was an old envelope; hand-printed across it were the words: "Open only upon my death."

"Here it is!" Gabe shouted to Mrs. Bell.

"You found something interesting?"

"Those guys are digging for buried treasure outside the window, but maybe I'm holding it here in my hand."

Mrs. Bell opened the envelope and read out loud what was written.

To Whom It May Concern: I write this in fear for my life. During a violent storm on the night of August 4, 1925, I picked up an SOS from a ship. There was nothing I could do, so rough was the Lake due to the storm. I could only signal back that the harbor was open. The ship went down at 4:27 a.m. I watched its lights sink into the violent waves. I noted this disaster in my log at daybreak, and informed the authorities on land.

I was later visited by an old salt who claimed he had been on that sailing ship and somehow made it to shore. I personally questioned his story. He claimed I had found the gold and had taken it. I had no idea of the ship's cargo and denied any knowledge of gold, and I denied taking anything. He threatened me with my life for lying to him and taking what was rightfully his.

I have not shared this with my wife. She would become hysterical and force us to leave the light. I would never leave because tending the light is my reason for being. Nor have I mentioned this to my children, as they would certainly tell their mother.

The sailor's name is Loren Scully. Though he is a lunatic, living a fantasy life as a pirate/hermit, he is exceptionally brilliant.

I ask forgiveness for my sins and claim Jesus Christ as my Lord and Savior. And, if the reader of this letter is someone other than my family, please tell my wife that I loved her very much, and also my children. I wish them all a long and happy life. Farewell, Lawrence Edwards, Keeper of the Squaw Island Light, August 15, 1925.

"Sounds like one mystery is solved," Gabe said, with a big smile on his face.

"Yes, it sure does," Mrs. Bell replied. "Mr. Kelly and Mr. Searing will enjoy this for sure."

"What a find! We'll share it with the others in Charlevoix and head home tomorrow."

Mrs. Bell immediately told Jack about the letter in the Bible. Not wanting to tamper the enthusiasm of the moment, Mrs. Bell said to Jack, "I wonder how the note got in the RV?"

"If it weren't a ghost, the only way I think it could happen is if that elderly lady in the library somehow got into the RV and put it there," Jack replied. "She may have known of the letter and its contents and wanted the news out, but maybe she didn't want to be the one to make it public?"

"Could be, but the motor home was either locked or occupied," Mrs. Bell said. "I'd swear that was the case."

From the beach came several shouts of joy. Apparently the diggers had hit something solid that wasn't a rock or driftwood. When they put their metal detectors down closer to the object the needle went crazy indicating something metal was under the sand.

They soon realized that it wasn't small. If they did unearth a treasure, the word would quickly spread and there would be no secret about what was in the sand. Eventually, the diggers unearthed a treasure chest just like those described and pictured in pirate movies or books. The chest had a lock on it. Justin brought the key he had found. In a most dramatic moment, Mr. Kelly tried to fit the key into the padlock, but as with unlucky contestants on television game shows, the key would not fit into the lock.

Mrs. Bell had the good sense to ask Mr. Kelly and get his advice about what should be done about it.

"I'd take the chest with us," Jack advised. "It is easier to say 'I'm sorry' after the fact if you've broken some scavenger law. Just keep good records of where it was found and take photos of the process."

The boat ride back to Charlevoix was smooth sailing. Once the treasure chest was moved to the RV, a feeling of great accomplishment enveloped everyone, students and adults alike.

Mrs. Bell and Ms. Scheiern asked the students to gather in the RV after dinner. "I have a surprise for you," Mrs. Bell began. "Only five of you could take our amazing trip out onto Lake Michigan on Mr. Tromp's boat. However, he has offered to take the rest of you for an evening cruise, so all of you can experience boating on Lake Michigan. How about that?"

"Cool!" said one of the students. The rest broke into a round of applause, and Jack knew that his suggestion had evoked great joy.

"We'll take the rest of you to the boat now, then we'll have a summary meeting tonight before lights-out, around ten."

A few minutes before ten, the entire group gathered for the summary of the trip. A light rain was falling as the eighteen students and two teachers reflected on the events of the last couple of days.

"First I'll read the letter Gabe found in the Bible at the light," Mrs. Bell said. After she finished, the students were very pleased that, presuming the perceived threat was real and Mr. Scully did kill him, Mr. Edwards' murder was now solved through his own words.

"But, an even greater mystery is, who put the note on the table in this RV?" Ms. Scheiern asked.

"Oh, it was probably Mr. Edwards — er, the ghost of Mr. Edwards," Mrs. Bell suggested. "The ghost probably wanted his murder solved after eighty-some years, and he figured another group of detectives would not come around for a long time."

"A ghost put a note there?" Ms. Scheiern said shivering. "No way! There are no such things as ghosts."

"But how could anyone living know that letter was in front of the book of Revelation?" Mrs. Bell asked. "There is absolutely no way! And, furthermore, we all agree the RV was locked when we were away. Now, unless Casper was a fluke, the only 'being' that can move through walls is a ghost. I mean, even Superman can't do it!"

"I agree," Ms. Scheiern replied. "There has to be some logical explanation. We just haven't hit on it yet. I know it will be explained!"

"Guess we're ready to go home," Jack said, trying to bring their attention from ghost talk back to reality.

"Yes, we need to do several things before we leave in the morning. I want a couple of you to write up a report for Mr. Searing. Use the computer and have it ready for Ms. Scheiern, Mr. Kelly, and myself to review.

"Someone needs to thank Mr. Tromp and his son for taking us to Squaw Island and for giving the rest of you a ride on Lake Michigan. Someone needs to write to Mrs. Angers. And finally, I need someone to write a thank-you note to the principal for allowing us to use the RV. When we get home we'll wash and clean this vehicle inside and out. It should be cleaner than when we drove it up here a few days ago. Ok, let's divvy up the work and get busy."

18

JULY 24

Lou was happy to be home in Grand Haven. He had been gone a couple of days and missed Carol, their dog, Samm, and Millie, their cat, and especially the sunset walks along the beach. Carol's quilt group met that evening, so their stroll on the shore would have to wait another day.

Lou went walking alone and found the effort therapeutic. Not only was it good exercise, but it was easy on the ears and eyes. At one point, Lou sat on a large piece of driftwood, thankful thoughts filling his mind. He was thankful for Carol, for his children, and grandchildren, for his friends, and for the opportunity to help people by solving some sticky crimes. But this investigation seemed quite cerebral. It hadn't been a shoot'em-up, chase-along-a-country-road investigation. This one had been close to drudgery — piecing together information, tossing out redundant theories, and hanging on to important facts.

Sitting on the piece of driftwood, he tried to put the facts together. The common element was the crossword puzzle on or near each body. But, how was there a connection when the Edwards and Bowman crimes had occurred more than eighty-five years apart? And, how could the 2007 murderer know of the 1925 murder to copy it? If there was a legitimate connection between the two crimes, perhaps generations of a family were involved; was there a Hatfield and McCoy rivalry involved? Or maybe the 2007 murderer was simply using a ploy similar to the 1925 event to throw off the police who would waste a lot of time digging up information that was totally irrelevant.

If this was a family battle, the victims would have to be connected beyond simply being people who were interested in lighthouses. Maybe Arthur Webberson was related to the keeper murdered in 1925. Or, maybe he was related to the murderer? Lou decided genealogical information for the past hundred years might be helpful, but obtaining it might be difficult.

By now, the sun had dropped into Wisconsin, or so it seemed, and Lou walked back toward home. He could see Samm waiting for him on the back porch, and he knew Carol would be home shortly, and then everything would be about as normal as possible. He passed neighbors having a fire on the beach, singing songs, as the guests, wearing sweatshirts and shorts, enjoyed this unique feature of living on the shore of Lake Michigan in the summertime.

The moon shone down upon the lake, now still except for the wakes of a few pleasure boats making their way to the channel and into their berths at harbors along the Grand River and in Spring Lake.

First, Lou gave Samm a brushing and allowed Millie to rub her head against his foot. Then he prepared a bowl of his favorite ice cream, Mackinac Island Fudge, turned on Tiger baseball, and waited for Carol to come home.

Alex Rodriguez was in the on-deck circle, the game with the White Sox tied in the 9th inning, when the phone rang. Lou was tempted to let the caller leave a message, but instead picked up the phone. It was Mrs. Bell calling from Charlevoix.

"Lou, I'm so glad to catch you. We have some very exciting news! Hope I'm not bothering you?"

"Oh no, just having some ice cream and watching the Tigers."

"Well, the students and I have become engrossed in this 1925 murder. Nobody seems to have paid much attention to this crime for almost eighty-three years. Maybe there was no official interest or concern, no expertise, we don't know, but it is almost like we came upon the scene soon after the crime occurred."

"What's your news?" Lou asked. "You've got me curious."

"Well, the kids and Mr. Kelly, who, by the way, has been worth his weight in gold, wanted me to call you. The place is filthy, spider webs all over, and mice dominate the place, but under all the filth is an intact home."

"That's strange. You'd think someone would need to keep operating the light."

"We think it's been maintained, but we don't think anybody lived there after the murder. It's as if the wife and children walked out and just never went back."

"So, below the dirt is a 1925 light as it was when the keeper's family lived there?"

"Exactly. We found a family Bible in the master bedroom and an envelope, oddly enough, at the beginning of the book of Revelation. On the front of the envelope was written, 'Only to be opened upon my death.' I'll read it to you."

Lou listened carefully until the letter was finished, then said, "This is fascinating. I'll bet you and the students felt like you had just discovered the lost civilization of Atlantis."

"We did, we surely did."

"Well, congratulations! You folks solved a crime," Lou exclaimed. "Great job!"

"Yes, we're pretty excited," Mrs. Bell replied. "Of course, there can be no justice unless this Scully guy is in the Guinness book as the longest-living person on earth."

"Now the job is to try and figure out a connection to the crossword puzzles," Lou mused aloud. "Someone must have known about this odd behavior and copied it. It can't have been happenstance."

"We agree. Jack concluded the same. Oh, one more thing. Do you believe in ghosts?" Mrs. Bell asked.

"I've not encountered one, but I suppose they're within the realm of possibility. Why?" Lou asked.

"Well, we were warned by a reliable source not to move anything in the light. We took the advice seriously, but it was hard not to move something, so we did. Ever since then, it is like we awakened a ghost, for strange things have been happening. I think the ghost of the light keeper has resided in that light since the murder."

"Maybe so, but what strange things?" Lou asked.

"A flat tire with no apparent puncture, or anything wrong with the valve; some food missing from the pantry in the RV; things being moved around, you know, odd stuff like that. Nothing life threatening — probably just a ghost nosing around."

"How are the kids about all of this?"

"All of what, discovering the letter?" Mrs. Bell asked.

"Well, yes, that, but I'm referring to the ghost, or the odd things happening."

"The kids are really 'up' about the letter — they have a story for life, helping you, and finding the solution to a mystery. But reactions to the strange happenings — a full range of behavior, from screams and panicking to laughter."

"Please tell them I am very proud of them," Lou said sincerely. "They are good detectives!"

"We knew you would be pleased."

"I am; most definitely, I am. Thank Jack as well."

"The kids love him, Lou. He was in the background, but he was the one who gently nudged them along. Actually, he's a bit more shaken by the strange happenings than the kids are."

"Don't worry. It's good for him to get a little riled from time to time."

During the telephone briefing, the ice cream had melted, and so had the Tigers, losing in the 10th after a hit with a man on second. Lou had missed the exciting conclusion to the game, but in the larger game of investigation, he seldom missed a thing. And now, some young folks from Greenville knew the joy of discovering connections and making sense of what was mysterious.

Carol was still not home. Lou had been away from his piano for a few days and felt like he needed that recreation. After going up and down the keyboard several times, once he felt his fingers were limber, he went right into a few of his favorites, like "Misty," songs from *Phantom of the Opera,* and songs from *The Sound of Music.* As he finished the last verse of "Do-Re-Mi," the garage door opened. Millie, the cat, made her way to the back door, and Samm barked once to announce that Carol was home. Now family was together, and all would be right with the world.

After Carol had a chance to wind down from the meeting, she and Lou went out onto the porch and sat beneath a million stars. The surf lapped rhythmically on the shore, a hundred or so feet away, as Lou and Carol took time to hear about one another's day.

217

"How is your investigation coming?" Carol asked.

"I'm almost finished with the tough work; you know, interviewing a slew of characters — and I do mean characters."

"How are Jack, those kids, and their teachers doing?"

"They're seeing more action at their fishing hole than I am. I got a call from Mrs. Bell this evening. They came across a document in the lighthouse that pretty much locks up the murder there."

"That's exciting."

"But, we still don't know whether the crossword puzzle resting on or near the bodies of both victims is a chance occurrence or a calculated move."

"I can't imagine it's chance," Carol said. "I mean, that would be almost impossible."

"I have a question for you," Lou said reaching over and taking Carol's hand.

"What's for dinner tomorrow?" Carol asked with a chuckle.

"No, not all of my life revolves around food."

"Even if that isn't your question, the answer is taco salad. I got all the makings at the city market this afternoon."

"Great, I love taco salad."

"That's precisely why I am planning on it for tomorrow. But, you had a question?"

"Yes. Would you like to go to London?"

"London, as in England, or London, as in Ontario?"

"I meant London, as in England."

"Why should we go to London?" Carol asked.

"I need to go for this case."

"Internet, e-mail, fax, and the telephone can't give you what you want?" Carol asked.

"They probably could, but I think I can be more thorough by going. I have a feeling I might find something to solve the Webberson mystery."

"Sure. I can shop in London, the food is good, and the museums are a delight. And I take advantage of every opportunity to get out of town."

"Great. The arrangements are all set. Pack your bag!"

The next morning before the students headed home to Greenville, Autumn Angers arrived at the campsite in Charlevoix. Mrs. Bell greeted her.

"I came to say goodbye," Mrs. Angers said with a smile

"Thanks. We really appreciated all of your help — the key, the history."

"I am glad I was able to help."

"More than help, you gave us access to the light. And that led to our solving this 1925 death for Mr. Searing."

"I really came to set the record straight." Mrs. Bell looked confused.

Mrs. Angers took a deep breath. "There is no ghost."

"No ghost — ?"

"I had some fun with all of you. I am an old woman, and I've held the secret long enough. While all of you were away from the RV, I had a locksmith let me in, and I put the note on the table."

"I knew there was some explanation!" Mrs. Bell exclaimed, relieved to know another mystery was solved. Some of the students moaned, wishing the ghost could survive so they could share that experience for a lifetime.

"I also let the air out of a tire and did some other things to indicate a 'spirit.' It was time to reveal the secret of Mr. Edwards' death. All these years I feared I would die before the truth could come out. I know of Mr. Searing, and I trust him. So, I really wanted to help you, to make sure people I could trust did the right thing with the story. But I couldn't help but have a little fun with you folks, to sort of liven up your adventure."

"You livened up our adventure, all right!" Mrs. Bell said with a laugh. "You had us going! But, thanks for coming out and explaining these strange events. I feel better now."

"I knew you would. Oh, one last thing. The chest of gold really does exist."

"It does?"

"Oh, yes, it's part of the story, a big part, but I'll leave that for another day."

"Please!" Mrs. Bell replied. "Don't leave us with another mystery."

"Mr. Scully and his descendents have no rightful claim to the gold. Rather, the gold belongs to the descendents of the lightkeeper's family. You take it from here."

Jack paid close attention and wrote down the information, planning to add it to his ever-growing case file.

Settled into their London hotel, Lou and Carol planned a day of sightseeing.

"I know you want to shop, and I want to make contacts here," Lou began. "So, I suggest we spend the first day doing what we need to do, and then we'll do the fun stuff."

"That's fine with me, but I came here to shop," Carol replied with a smile.

"For me, it's investigating, so I guess that's my priority."

"I agree with that. But, before we do anything else, we need to try to find tickets for a show tonight."

Lou picked up his files. "I'll check with the concierge on my way out, unless you want to do that."

"I'll do the checking," Carol said, "and get tickets for what I think we'll enjoy."

"Good. With my ears, you'll need to tell me all about it afterwards anyway. But, the more color, dancing, and unique staging, the better."

"I'll see that we get a good show, and I'll get us as close to the stage as possible."

"Don't pay too much, now."

"Oh, Lou, lighten up! We're in London and have a chance for live theater. We can't take it with us," Carol argued.

"Right, but there is a limit, and we may need it while we're here."

"I'll take care of the show, and you go investigate. How's that?"

"Okay, I'm heading for the records office to see if I can find anything about Arthur Webberson," Lou said.

"And, I'm going to Harrods," Carol replied. "Tally ho, Lou."

"Whatever, my dear Carol."

Before leaving for London, Lou had determined where vital records were kept and had made an appointment with Miss Ann Liming, a librarian in the genealogy department of the London Public Library. This would be his first stop.

Lou stopped at the front desk. "I have an appointment with Miss Liming. I'm here to locate information about a man by the name of Arthur S. Webberson."

"Are you familiar with computers?" the receptionist asked.

"Yes, but what might take me four hours could take considerably less time with some help."

"I see. Miss Liming will be with you shortly."

"Thank you."

After about ten minutes of enjoyable people watching, a smiling woman approached Lou.

"Miss Liming, I presume?"

"Yes. I'm pleased to meet you, Mr. Searing."

"I am trying to find anything you might have on Arthur S. Webberson — birth, marriage, anything."

"You have only his name? No city, village, borough?"

"No."

"Age, approximate date of birth or marriage?"

"He is 65 years old, so I guess he would have been born in 1941 or 1942."

"Hmmm, that may pose a problem. We lost some records in the war years, but we'll see what we can do."

"Thank you." Lou watched as the aide went to work, efficiently tapping into the records system. Behind his back, he had his fingers crossed for something that would shed new light on the case.

"We show twenty-five A. Webbersons in the London census of 1950. That's a start."

"Yes, thank you." Lou replied.

"We can break that down further: six Aarons, two Abrahams, one Aristotle, four Andrews, eight Arthurs, and four with only the initial 'A.' So, we have identified eight Arthur Webbersons. Now, let's see what happens with that middle initial." A few seconds later Ann said, "Now, we are down to two."

"Great job! I really appreciate your help."

"This is what makes this job enjoyable," Ann replied. "You're from the States?"

"Yes, Michigan."

"Oh, that's the mitten state, right?"

"Well, yes, the Lower Peninsula has a mitten shape. The Yoopers don't like that, because they're cut off when you refer to Michigan as a mitten. Most residents would either like to be independent, or they'd prefer to join Wisconsin, a bordering state."

"What did you say, 'Yoopers'?"

"It's plural for those in the Upper Peninsula, U.P. — Yoopers."

"I see. Anyway, Michigan's an interesting place."

"Thank you; I think so."

Considering the information on the computer screen, Ann remarked, "Now, I show an Arthur Sidney Webberson, and an

Arthur S. Webberson; both are 65. Sidney's parents were Harold Webberson and Gretta Hollingworth. The other Webberson's father was Sir Jonathan Webberson — a little royalty there, it appears. But, his mother is not listed. Which did you want?"

"Both, actually, but I think the man I'm looking for is Arthur S. Webberson."

"Unless you can prove that you are related, I can't give you a copy of the record. You can write down the information, however." Lou quickly took copious notes.

"May I ask if you show a marriage for Arthur S. Webberson?"

"Let's see." The computer keys tapped rapidly and soon Lou heard, "Yes, Arthur S. Webberson married Irma Roberts on first of May, 1963, in London."

"That's great," Lou said, excited at these developments. "Is there any record of his having children?"

A moment later, the aide said, "He is the father of Andrew S. Webberson, who was born in 1967."

"Anything else on this man?" Lou asked.

"I'll see. Here is one last reference. He and his wife placed a son, Andrew in an orphanage when he was less than a year old because of severe retardation. The City of London took over guardianship for the lad."

"Okay, let me finish writing this down and I'll be on my way. Does the record indicate what orphanage accepted the boy?"

"Yes, the Manchester Orphanage."

"Thanks so much. You've been very helpful."

"Glad I could help you."

"If you ever come to the States and want a tour of Michigan, give me a ring, or drop me a line. Here is my card."

"Thank you. Where are you staying?"

"The River Thames Hotel."

"Oh yes, a grand place. Very hospitable. Enjoy your time in London."

"Thank you."

Lou remembered her comment about "…a bit of royalty there…" He knew that the Metropolitan Police, better known to many as Scotland Yard, would have information regarding the Royal family.

Lou took a taxicab to Scotland Yard. There he found the same courtesy that he encountered at the London Public Library. Once again an employee was willing to assist.

"I'm looking for information concerning the marriage of an Arthur S. Webberson," Lou said.

"Here we go, sir. We don't show a marriage, but we show a civil ceremony linking Mr. Webberson to Lady Wellsley in July of 1963."

"Not a wedding?"

"No, I suspect there was a bit of a cover-up, which often happens with royalty. Mr. Webberson and Lady Wellsley had a child out of wedlock, Andrew, who suffered from some abnormality. So, he was placed in an orphanage, becoming a ward of the City of London."

"I see. At the public library, in the genealogical section, they show a marriage to a woman named Irma Roberts, May 1, 1963."

"Public records are sometimes falsified to prevent scandal. I suspect Lady Wellsley was a mistress. If he was not married, they had a moment of indiscretion, as we say, and they were probably discouraged from marrying, as he was not of royal blood. I'm sure you understand."

"This Lady Wellsley — where does she fit into the royal line?"

"Quite a way back, I'm afraid. She is related to the Queen, but so far back and sideways that one might never hear of her."

Carol was having a most enjoyable time in Harrods, shopping for the Searing children and grandchildren. The most difficult aspect of shopping was trying to find correct sizes. She needed a chart to show metric units versus English units. After all, there would be no exchanging anything. She got Lou some chocolate, knowing his love for special treats. This was pure Carol, shopping for family and close friends. She had more time before she was to meet Lou so she went to Liberty, an historic store that was something to behold. She also found several high-quality fabrics to share with her quilting friends back home.

That evening, Lou and Carol enjoyed a delicious meal in the River Thames Hotel. Everything was purely British, from the décor to the food. After dinner, they took a cab to the London Theater to see Agatha Christie's *The Mousetrap*. It was marvelous from beginning to end. The seats were front-and-center, and Lou heard every word.

In the lobby during intermission, the two threw all caution to the wind as they kissed and hugged one another. "Here we are in London. Can you believe it?" Lou asked. "This almost beats a walk on the shore, don't you think?"

"For sure. We're blessed, Lou. We are truly blessed."

After the show, Lou and Carol caught a cab to the hotel. Before going in, they took a short walk to enjoy views of the Thames, Big Ben, and the lights of London. It was truly a magical evening!

The Searings spent the morning of the second day sight-seeing. High on the list was a tour of Westminster Abbey, the Tower of London, and Trafalgar Square, which, as far as Lou was concerned, was simply an over-publicized traffic circle. But it was a landmark and worthy of seeing since they were in London.

To give Lou some balance, Carol made sure that they took the Tube to the northern part of London to visit Madame Tussauds Wax Museum. She took Lou's photo standing beside Sherlock Holmes and Dr. Watson. Lou thought he had died and gone to heaven.

Mid-afternoon of the second day, Lou hailed a cab and directed the driver to the Manchester Orphanage. There he asked the records attendant for files on Andrew Webberson, admitted in 1967. As at the Public Records Office, Lou could not have copies of records, but the administrator allowed him to look through the file on Andrew.

The file was uninformative until he came upon a series of receipts. An envelope was attached to a copy of a check with a note, *"For the care of Andrew Webberson."* The return address was a holiday address label which read, *"Arthur and Abigail Dickenson, 14366 South Wickman Dr., Lima, Ohio."*

"Andy has Savant Syndrome and can play entire piano concertos after hearing one performance," the orphanage administrator told Lou. "He needs round-the-clock care because he has the intelligence of a four-year-old, but his piano-playing is virtuoso level."

"Is that so?"

"Yes, he is quite famous, at least among those who appreciate classical pianists."

"Do you know where he lives? Do you know his guardian?"

"I've heard that he lives in what you in America would call a group home, but I don't know where it is." Lou thanked the administrator and returned to his hotel where he immediately e-mailed Miss Wilber at the Gratiot County CAC office, asking for the e-mail address of the person she had contacted concerning Andrew Webberson.

Then Lou sent an e-mail to Jack Kelly. It read, "Jack, please find out what you can about an Arthur and Abigail Dickenson of Lima, Ohio. E-mail me as soon as you learn anything. He apparently sent money to a London orphanage for his son, Andrew Webberson. Two and two are not making four, and I need to reconcile the notion of two fathers of one son. Carol and I are having a great time in London! We'll be back in Michigan soon. Lou."

Miss Wilber replied with the e-mail address Lou needed. Lou immediately typed a message to Andrew's guardian. "Greetings. My name is Lou Searing, and I am trying to find Andrew Webberson, the gifted pianist. I have information about his father that may be of interest to him." He hit the send key and hoped for a response.

Shortly, Jack replied to Lou. "Apparently, Arthur Webberson had the last name of Dickenson when he lived in Lima, Ohio. His wife was Abigail and his adult children are Alice and Arnold. Hope this helps, Lou."

About an hour passed before Lou received a reply from Henry Postwaite, the caregiver for Andrew Webberson. "I don't know from where you sent the message, Mr. Searing, but you are welcome to visit. If you are in London, our address is 555 Buckinghamshire Court. If you are out of London, you may call on the telephone, 555-393-7651. I look forward to hearing from you."

Lou immediately replied, "I will be at your door within the hour. Thanks so much." Lou left a note for Carol, and hurriedly hailed a taxicab, forgetting his umbrella though a steady rain was falling.

The taxi darted in and around traffic, and, in what seemed no time at all, arrived at 555 Buckinghamshire Court. "This shouldn't take long. Could you wait for me?"

"Aye, lad. Take your time."

Lou thanked him, walked up to the door and knocked.

"Mr. Searing?" a tall man of about thirty asked.

"Yes."

"Do come in. My name is Henry Postwaite. May I serve you tea or coffee?"

"No thanks. I have the taxi waiting, as I don't think this will take long."

"Would you like to meet Andrew?" Henry asked.

"Most definitely. Does he understand who I am or why I'm here?"

"No. He would not comprehend it, sir."

"I see."

The two men entered a bright room. A grand piano was positioned in the middle of an undecorated room. A couch sat against the wall opposite a bay window. An elaborate sound system stood to one side. "Andrew spends most of his time in here. Actually he spends most of his waking hours playing and listening to music."

Lou looked at Andrew and immediately noticed a striking resemblance to the allegedly deceased Mr. Webberson. Lou approached Andrew and put out his hand, but Andrew didn't respond. He looked tense, apparently stressed by the interruption.

Lou turned to his host, "I can leave now. Thank you."

Once the two men had left the room, Lou asked, "Andrew's father and mother — are they living?"

"I believe his mother is alive and living here in England. I don't know anything about his father."

"I see."

"Was his father Arthur S. Webberson? Lou asked.

"Yes."

"What does the S. stand for, if I may ask?"

"The official records state that Andrew's father's middle name was Scully."

"Spelled S-K?" Lou wanted to be sure.

"No, S-C-U-L-L-Y," Henry replied, emphasizing the C.

"Thank you," Lou said. "Here's my card. If you should learn anything more about Mr. Arthur S. Webberson, I would appreciate your letting me know."

"I will do that, sir."

Lou thanked Mr. Postwaite for hosting his visit, and for the opportunity to see Andrew and to learn Arthur's middle name. The two shook hands. Lou walked to the cab and asked to go back to the hotel.

"Was the trip worth your time, mate?" the cabbie asked.

"Yes, most definitely."

"Young Webberson is an amazing talent."

"You know of him?" Lou asked.

"Londoners do, aye."

"Actually I am more interested in his father than in Andrew."

"Left the boy in the orphanage as a baby, I understand."

"Yes, I know."

Having decided that the trip to London had been well worth the time and money, Lou and Carol returned on a trans-Atlantic flight to Chicago, and then a puddle-jumper up to Grand Rapids from O'Hare.

Once belongings were unpacked, Millie and Samm brought home from the neighbors', mail and newspapers collected, and phone and e-mail messages reviewed, Lou and Carol took their evening stroll along the beach.

After a hundred or so feet of walking along the packed, wet sand, Carol asked, "So, the trip was worthwhile for your case, I take it?"

"Yes, it was. I think we may be getting close to solving this thing. I'm anxious to talk to Jack."

Lou's cell phone rang. He answered it, "Lou, this is Jack. Welcome home, stranger."

"Well, thanks for calling. I just told Carol I was anxious to talk to you. I got some good information which I am looking forward to sharing with you."

"And, I'm looking forward to hearing it. I have a theory, and if you give me the right answers, I think we'll have this thing wrapped up."

"We can talk in detail when Carol and I finish our walk, or you can drive down here."

"I'll drive down." Jack offered. "I'll be there in 20 minutes."

"Ok, see you soon." Lou put the phone in his pocket, took Carol's hand and they continued walking along the shore as bright stars replaced a colorful western sunset.

19

While Carol watched *The Amazing Race* on television, Lou and Jack gathered all of their notes at the far end of the dining room table, believing that within the stack of papers were enough facts to make sense of this murder or disappearance.

"Can I get you something to drink, Jack?"

"I don't want anything with caffeine."

"How about a caffeine free Diet Pepsi?" Lou asked.

"Sounds good, and if you've a few M & Ms, I'll not turn them down either."

"Oh sure, we've got some of those. Some of my best thinking goes on with sugar cavorting through my veins."

"Chocolate and a diet — we're set to go!" Jack said with a chuckle.

"Okay, whodunit, Jack? Give it your best shot."

"Well, I've given this a lot of thought. Let's approach this from who I don't think did it."

"Works for me," Lou replied.

"It was not Rose," Jack began. "She's smart enough not to let her anger over not getting a lighthouse put her in the slammer. And it was not Wally or any other member of the family. I think…"

"Excuse me for interrupting," Lou said. "I agree with you so far. I showed a photo of Rose, Florence, Wally's wife Bea, and Victoria to the maintenance man at the Kammeraad Funeral home and he couldn't identify any of them as the woman who picked up the body. "But, I can't seem to let go of Jenny," Lou continued. "She lied to me, and you recall, that's one of your rules."

"I know. I also don't think it is anyone connected with the HOMES Lighthouse Association."

"Again, I agree," Lou remarked. "The one possible suspect is Norman Root, and he's just a guy who usually says the wrong thing at the wrong time."

Jack continued with his analysis. "Now, originally I thought Ted might have been involved. You recall, I gave him high marks for intelligence, and I felt he would figure into this in some way. For a while I thought he might very well have arranged the murder of his brother. He had buffaloed people into thinking he had Alzheimer's, or dementia, and that would rule him out for all practical purposes. He would have had his revenge, sparked by jealousy of his brother's success, and so I had him high on my list."

"What pushed him off?" Lou asked.

"Money — or lack of it. I looked into his finances as deeply as I could, and he appears to have a small military pension besides Social Security to live on. And that money goes directly to the home that cares for him. No hit man would do this for nothing. So, Ted went off the list."

"So, who's left?" Lou wanted to know.

"I don't have a name, but I have a theory."

"So do I, and my guess is we have the same theory," Lou remarked, popping two dark blue M & Ms into his mouth. "Go ahead."

"I think we're seeing a family feud that was never resolved."

"I knew that was what you were going to say!" Lou remarked, slapping his palm on the table. "Go on."

"I think that people related to Edwards, the lighthouse keeper, and those related to Scully, the pirate mentioned in the lighthouse keeper's letter, are still at odds over the alleged chest of gold."

"So, if you're right, we need genealogical charts."

"Correct," Jack said. "And I've started to put them together."

"Great. What have you found?"

"Well, it doesn't solve the murder, but it offers new suspects," Jack replied. "As best I can determine, there are two survivors on the keeper's side: a man named Elmer Edwards, and his daughter Ruth Botsford, who lives in Oregon."

"Allow me to sing along, Jack," Lou replied, anxious to be a part of the theory. "The living relatives on the pirate's side are Arthur Scully Webberson and his ancestors."

"Probably. So, this pirate, Scully, must have had a daughter who married a Webberson. They must have had a son who becomes Sir Jonathan Webberson who resided in England. His sons must be Theodore and Arthur S. Webberson," Jack surmised.

"So, if we're right, Elmer Edwards could have murdered Arthur Webberson," Lou concluded.

"Yes and the accomplice who picked up the body at the funeral home was probably Ruth Botsford," Jack concluded. "BINGO!"

"What about Frieda Bowman?" Lou asked. "Do you think there is a connection, or is that case totally separate?"

"Don't know. Let's take these one at a time," Jack suggested.

"Something is nagging at me," Lou replied. "Let me go through my notes quickly. Help yourself to more pop and M & Ms, but please don't interrupt me. I don't want to lose this thought."

Lou turned page after page, looking for something that fit into their discussion. After about five minutes, Lou said, "Here it is. Listen. A while ago I got a voice message, probably from the killer. Part of what he said is, 'One more thing: ask yourself why Professor Wilkenson finds it necessary to begin his lecture by telling the audience about a murder'."

"Who's Professor Wilkenson?" Jack asked.

"I don't know for sure. I'll call Mr. Hicks of the HOMES Association in the morning."

"There has to be some significance in the crossword puzzles, Lou."

"My guess is it's the words with missing letters."

"Obviously, but the words go across and up-and-down. Which way offers the clues?" Lou asked.

"Got me. Let's put all the letters on the table and see if in unscrambling them, something makes sense."

Onto the table went sticky notes with the letters G, R, E, V, N, E. For the next couple of minutes the two men pretended to play Scrabble until Jack blurted out, "REVENGE."

"That works, and that's what my son thought," Lou replied. "But we're one letter short. Even if it is 'revenge,' it really doesn't help us. All of the suspects could be seeking revenge."

"Maybe the key isn't the letters that are missing, but either the completed word or the clues," Jack suggested.

"Ok, let's see what we can get from those."

"The words are; POWER, NEVER, UNDERESTIMATE, and GREED," Jack recalled.

"Maybe it's simple: 'Never underestimate the power of greed'," Lou concluded.

"Actually, if you only use the four words, you get, 'Never underestimate power greed'."

"Right, either the adjective 'the', and preposition 'of', are understood, or..."

"There are more deaths to come," Jack said.

"Exactly."

Lou suddenly remembered Mary telling him that the word in the next puzzle was "the." "I'm going to call Miss Wilber in the morning as well. Mary, Rose McCracken's sister, knows more than she told us."

After breakfast, Lou called Julian Hicks. "Mr. Searing, how can I help you?"

"I'm trying to find out about a man name Wilkenson. Does that name ring a bell?"

"He's a well-known lighthouse researcher and historian, Lou. Dr. Leonard Wilkenson lectures all over the country. Why are you interested in him, if I may ask?"

"His name came up in our investigation into the murder of Arthur Webberson."

"Not as a suspect, I hope?"

"No, but he apparently begins some lectures with references to one or more lighthouse murders, and I'm curious why."

"I have a lot of ways to contact him. Which would you like?" Julian asked.

"The one with the highest chance of reaching him quickly."

"In that case, I'll give you his cell phone. Whenever I call him, he either answers or quickly returns my call."

"Thanks," Lou said, jotting down the phone number.

"While you are on the line, how are you coming on the case?" Julian asked. "About to solve it, are you?"

"We're getting closer. I am hoping this Wilkenson fellow can take us to the next level in the investigation."

"Good luck."

Lou then called Gloria Wilber at the Gratiot County CAC office. "Good morning, Lou. What's happening?"

"I want to ask about Mary," Lou began. "She is an enigma. She has information that may help our investigation, but I can't figure out where it's coming from."

"We wonder the same thing from time to time," Gloria replied. "Can you give me an example of what you've heard?"

"She told me the word in the next puzzle is 'the.' Actually that is very possible in this case, but if she didn't know all the other words in puzzles found at the death scenes, she wouldn't know that 'the' holds any significance."

"All I can tell you is that there is no way she could get any information here at the center. I mean, she could have heard something from someone else, but there is nothing to read. We do post newspaper articles about the case, but they don't provide specifics."

"Is she capable of going on the Internet and researching?"

"No, she isn't. If a friend finds something interesting, she might look at the computer screen, but I've never seen her initiate any activity herself, or talk about using the Internet."

"Where is she living now? Do you know, or are you not at liberty to tell me?"

"I do know, but I can't tell you."

"Even if it might save someone's life?" Lou asked.

"I can't Lou — she asked for my confidence. I can tell her how important this is and ask her permission to tell you. Or, I suppose you could follow her home after one of our meetings. I can't control that. Excuse me Lou, I've got to take another call. It is important, but please stay on the line."

"Sure."

A few minutes later Gloria was back with Lou. "Well, that sure is a coincidence. The man on the phone was one of Mary's caretakers. He'd like to talk with you because Mary has been saying disturbing things. I hope it is okay, because I gave him your number."

"Perfect. Thanks so much. I'll hang up and wait for his call. Who will I be talking to?" Lou asked, pen in hand.

"His name is Hal Bate."

Within a minute, Lou's cell phone rang. "Hello. Lou Searing here."

"Mr. Searing, this is Hal Bate from Alma."

"Yes, Miss Wilber said you might call."

"I know you are investigating the murder of some lighthouse man, whose name escapes me at the moment."

"Arthur Webberson."

"Yes. You are probably not specifically aware that Mary McCracken is living with us. She has been mistreated by her sister, and the sister is threatening to take her away from the area. Mary does not want to be mistreated, or to leave her friends. So, we are helping her."

"I see. Has the abuse been reported?" Lou asked, knowledgeable about required procedures.

"No. I don't think she wants to report it. I think it was a one-time thing, but it caused her to be uncomfortable around her sister."

"How can I help you?" Lou asked.

"Mary is, shall I say, obsessed with this murder. She seems to make up stories, and lately she claims she knows who has done the killing. She supposedly knows who will be next. It's at the point where I think I might be liable if I don't tell someone about her stories, because maybe they are true, and maybe someone is going to be killed."

"That's wise. Where is she getting the information?" Lou asked.

"I don't know. She has a part-time maintenance job at Alma College, so maybe people are telling her things there. Or, maybe she is clairvoyant. I don't know."

"Did you ask her where she is getting this information?" Lou asked.

"Yes, but she says either she doesn't know or she's forgotten where she heard it."

"Do you know where she works at the college?"

"At the Student Union and in the cafeteria," Hal replied.

"I'll go to the college and ask around — maybe something will pop up. Meanwhile, if you hear anything else, don't hesitate to let me know, any time of the day or night."

"I will. Thank you, Mr. Searing."

It turned into a morning on the phone. Next up was a call to Dr. Wilkenson. Lou dialed the number, expecting to get a "Sorry I am not able to take your call right now…," but a gentleman answered. "Hello."

"Dr. Wilkenson?"

"Speaking."

"This is Lou Searing in Michigan. I am an investigator looking into the murder of Mr. Arthur Webberson. May I have a few minutes to ask a couple of questions?"

"I'm very busy and really don't think I have anything to help you. Thanks for calling…"

"Wait, wait, sir. Please give me a couple of minutes," Lou pleaded. "I received a phone message shortly after the murder and the caller specifically asked me to wonder why you choose to begin your talk with information about a lighthouse murder. Do you usually do that?"

"It depends where I am. I think you are referring to the lecture I gave in Bailey's Harbor, Wisconsin, a beautiful area by the way. I'm sure that is the conference in question. I began that talk with a description of a lighthouse murder near Munising because of two men in my audience. Their lives, probably unbeknownst to them, intertwine with murder in a lighthouse."

"Please go on," Lou responded.

"I didn't mention specifics, and I didn't name the murder that involves them indirectly, but I may have put a match to a long fuse."

"What is the connection?"

"A man in the audience, a Mr. Elmer Edwards, is two generations removed from Lawrence Edwards, the lighthouse keeper who was killed on Squaw Island. Also in the audience was an Arthur Webberson, who is related to the alleged murderer, whose last name was Scully. I saw them talking a few times during the conference. I don't know what they discussed, but I found it odd that they were connecting, and I wondered whether they knew of the violence in 1925 that linked their families. Also, has a Ruth Botsford come up in your work?"

"Yes, she's been mentioned," Lou replied.

"Then you know that she is Elmer Edwards' daughter. She lives in Portland, Oregon, and she has the gold. Not many people know this, of course."

"Does the name Frieda Bowman mean anything to you?" Lou asked.

"Oh my yes, she was the hostess of that conference in Door County, Wisconsin. She is a great student of lighthouses, and she leads many tours in the Great Lakes area. In fact, she and Mr. Edwards got into a heated exchange during my talk in Door County."

"What do you mean?"

"Mr. Edwards wanted to talk about the murder of his grandfather on Squaw Island, but Miss Bowman would not allow it. She snapped at him, and he at her. It became ugly, and most of the other participants were uncomfortable."

"Who could give me contact information for those attending your lecture in Wisconsin?" Lou asked.

"Frieda Bowman certainly could."

"I gather you haven't heard that Miss Bowman was murdered in Manistee last July third."

"Oh, my. No, I had not heard. I did hear that Mr. Webberson had been killed, but I was led to believe that murder was committed by a family member, jealous of an inheritance."

"Where did you hear this?" Lou inquired.

"From Ruth Botsford."

"The woman in Oregon, Mr. Edwards' daughter?"

"Yes."

"Do you know where I could find a photograph of Mrs. Botsford?" Lou asked.

"Actually I do. The HOMES Association would have one. Are you familiar with them?" Dr. Wilkenson asked.

"Yes, I've dealt with them during my investigation."

"They put out an annual report. Ruth Botsford's picture is in that report as one of the founders, and last year they specifically honored the founders. So, if you can get a copy of that annual report, it's near the front. I can't get over Frieda being murdered. Is it true that Mr. Webberson was killed by a family member?"

"The investigation is on-going, but I will tell you that we have no direct evidence that a family member is the murderer."

"Thank you. I'm glad you called. I hope my information has been helpful."

"Most definitely. Thank you."

Lou needed to charge his phone before making another call. An hour later he called Mr. Hicks of the HOMES Association. "Julian, this is Lou Searing."

"Yes, Lou."

"Could you copy and fax to me the page with pictures of your founders in your last annual report?"

"Sure. You'll have it in five minutes. Then I'll send the entire report overnight express and you'll have it in the morning."

Lou gave him the fax number, and Julian assured him the page would be on its way.

"One more question. Does your membership list include a Theodore Webberson?"

"Yes, it does."

"Is there also an Elmer Edwards?"

"Yes."

"Do all members get your annual report?"

"Certainly."

"Thank you. I'll look for your fax."

Next Lou called Jack. A woman answered, "Hello."

"Elaine?"

"Yes, Mr. Searing?"

"Yes. I am calling for Jack. Is he in?"

"He's right here. Jack is certainly enjoying working with you."

"He's a big help."

"I'm sure he is. He's a very intelligent man. Here he is."

Ten seconds later Lou heard, "Hi, Lou."

"Well, partner, things are heating up. This one is almost in the bag."

"Great. What did you learn?" Jack asked.

"First, here is what I would like you to do."

"Sounds like you're off to slay another windmill."

"Probably. Please, if you can, go to Alma College and find out how Mary McCracken is learning things about our investigation. She works in maintenance, assigned to the student center and the cafeteria. See what you can find, okay?"

"I'm on my way. Now tell me what you've learned."

For the next few minutes Lou summarized his phone calls, his new information, and his new theory about who killed Frieda and Arthur. Both Lou and Jack felt good about wrapping this up.

20

While Jack headed to Alma College, Lou drove to Reed City to talk with Kenneth James, maintenance man at the Kammeraad Funeral Home. Ken received permission to break from his work to talk with Lou. The two decided to go to Starbucks in town, so they went in Lou's car, making small talk along the way.

Once settled with their coffee, Lou began. "I'm convinced the solution to this murder lies in the delivery and pick-up of the body at your funeral home. The crossword puzzles are clues, and we've gathered other helpful facts, but it seems to me, the solution lies with you."

"Wow! I've never been involved with anything this important. I wish I could help, but I've answered all of your questions honestly. I don't know what more I can do."

"You recall when I showed you some photos a week or so ago, I showed you the Webberson family picture, and you looked at Arthur's wife, his daughter, and his daughter-in-law."

"Yes. And none of them looked like the woman who dropped off the body."

"Right," Lou said. "And then I showed you a picture from a high school yearbook."

"Right, and she didn't look like the woman either."

"I have two more photos I'd like you to look at."

"Okay."

"This is one of the founders of the HOMES Lighthouse Association. Do you recognize her as the person who dropped off the body?" Ken held the photo briefly.

"There is a resemblance, but I don't think so. She's older than the woman I saw."

"Okay, here's another picture. This is the woman in the yearbook eight or nine years later. She's a bit heavier in this photo, and her hairstyle is different." Lou put the photo in front of Ken.

"I suppose this could be her. She had on a hat and sunglasses remember, and I was preoccupied helping with the body. If someone had said, 'Take a good look at this woman, because you'll need to identify her later,' I would have paid more attention."

"I understand."

"But, this woman does look about the same size, same height as the woman who dropped off the body."

"But, you can't be one hundred percent certain?" Lou tried giving Ken some slack.

"No, I can't, but I am one hundred percent certain of something else."

"What's that?"

"The vehicle in the photo, behind the woman. It's just like the vehicle which came to the delivery door."

Surprised, Lou asked, "What makes you so sure?"

"My wife and I had been looking at SUVs, mainly a certain vehicle, same make, style, and even color, so I paid attention to it. As I recall, I even asked the woman if she was happy with it."

"And, what did she say?"

"She said she had just gotten it, so she really couldn't give me an honest opinion."

The two men finished their coffee, and Lou drove Mr. James back to the funeral home expressing appreciation for Ken's time and memory.

Jack easily found the Student Union and Cafeteria on the Alma campus. He recognized Mary immediately and saw that she appeared to be responsible for the back half of the cafeteria, and her job was bussing tables. Jack sat near the front and watched her work, pretending to read a book. Occasionally she would stop and sit down with some students, but not for long.

In the middle of the dinner hour, Jack noticed that Mary seemed especially pleased when two coeds put their trays down on a table in her section. Mary immediately stopped her work to talk with them. The discussion seemed serious. Jack moved to an adjoining table. He heard some of the conversation and with his speech reading skill, was able to put some sentences together.

When Mary took her cart full of dirty dishes to the kitchen, Jack approached the two students and introduced himself. "Excuse me, may I join you?"

"I guess so."

"I'm embarrassed to say this, but I saw you two talking to the lady bussing the tables and forgive my intrusion, but I am pretty good at speech reading. Did I see one of you say something about a murder?"

"I did. We were talking to Mary about what we've read on a blog about the murder in Ludington. My brother went up to Squaw Island with some classmates to help solve the crime."

"I see — that clarifies it. Again, I am very sorry to intrude on your dinner, but I couldn't help wondering why the word 'murder' would be part of a conversation on a college campus like this."

"No problem. Because of my brother's involvement, we often look at an Internet blog called 'unsolved mysteries,' and it's really cool."

"Yeah," the second girl interjected. "Right now the hot thing is the lighthouse murders. People who have access to the blog post theories for others to read. It's kind of neat. We check it daily to see the latest guess as to what might happen. Then at dinner, when Mary is working, she's real curious about it because she likes lighthouses and goes on many tours with her sister, Dr. McCracken."

"I see. I didn't know there was a blog about unsolved mysteries," Jack replied.

"Yeah, what's really fun is predicting what will happen next. For example, one person said he thinks the letters in the puzzles form a major clue. Someone else predicts another murder at a lighthouse in southwest Michigan. Things like that. Afterward, we read the newspapers to see if any of these predictions really came true."

"It adds some excitement," replied the second girl.

"Thanks for the info. Again, sorry for the interruption."

"No problem."

In his car headed to Muskegon, Jack called Lou on his cell and reported what he had learned.

"Good work, Jack! I hesitated to ask you to go because I thought it would be a long trip for little gain, but the detective gods were with us, I guess."

"I didn't know there were blogs that followed investigations," Jack said.

"I've heard of them, but I've never paid them much attention. Seems I'm always a step ahead on my cases, and they're just amateur sleuths taking stabs at possible suspects and motives. Kind of boring, and certainly a waste of my time."

"Right."

"But, it does explain where Mary is getting the information she's sharing with her caregivers. It's not clairvoyance — she's just passing on blog stuff. Good job, Jack! Thank you very much."

"You're welcome. Do you have anything new for me?"

"Actually, I do. Jenny just may be involved in this thing. The maintenance man at the Kammeraad Funeral Home said the recent photo of Jenny could be the woman he saw, but he is sure the SUV in the picture is identical to the vehicle that delivered the body."

"Maybe she is involved. I thought not, but maybe," Jack admitted. "Where do we go from here, Lou?"

"Elmer Edwards. Dr. Wilkenson saw him talking to Arthur a few times at a conference in Wisconsin. He might have a story to tell. I'm going to try to reach him, and when I interview him, I'd like you along."

"I'll be there, hero of mine."

"OK. Later, Jack."

21

Lou's cell phone rang. "Lou Searing here."

"Lou? Mickey McFadden."

"Yes, Mickey. I've been meaning to call you, to bring you up-to-date with what Jack and I have learned."

"Guess I beat you to it. I've got new information about the Bowman murder. A citizen came forward who remembered seeing a couple of people pushing a wheelbarrow out onto the pier on July 3rd. She's a cottage owner who couldn't sleep and decided to take a walk on the beach. It was the middle of the night, and she thought it odd."

"I'd think it odd too. Could she follow their activities?" Lou asked.

"Apparently not," Mickey replied. "That is all she saw — two people pushing a wheelbarrow onto the pier."

"But, why put the body up on the catwalk, Mickey? I can see taking the body out on the pier, tying a cinder block to it, and dumping it into the channel, or even just leaving it on the pier, but why go to all that effort? The body is dead weight — excuse the pun — and for what? If they needed to hide the body, there are a million places to take it rather than the catwalk over a pier."

"True. There must to be some reason for it," Mickey, replied. "I agree, it's illogical to put it there if the murderer wanted us to think it was a natural death."

"Absolutely. How many people climb up onto a catwalk and then have a heart attack?"

"Right. Well, I'll leave you to ponder that. What the person saw may not relate to the Bowman murder, but I wanted you to know about it."

"Thanks, and while you are on the line, let me bring you up to speed on the Webberson murder."

In the stack of mail Carol picked up on her way home from shopping was a letter addressed to Lou. "You've got some mail!" Carol shouted to Lou, who was working in his office on the second floor.

"Be right there."

Lou came downstairs, gave Carol a kiss on the cheek. "Good shopping trip?"

"Yes. I stopped by the post office and chatted with Marion Smith, the 'Postal Goddess,' as she likes to be called. She noticed you hadn't been picking up your mail. She told me you need to come on in because she's put some chocolate candy in your P.O. Box. I tell you, Lou, lots of people are looking after you."

"Pretty lucky guy, me!" Lou replied smiling.

Lou picked up the letter. "Looks like something from a law office. Hope I'm not getting sued." He opened it and read, "Dear Mr. Searing. It appears we have something in common: we are looking for the same man. You are seeking Arthur S. Webberson, and I am searching for Arthur S. Dickenson. Could we meet to combine our resources in hopes of reaching our mutual goals? By the way, he is not dead." Included was a business card from Joseph Day, with a Lima, Ohio, mailing and e-mail address.

Lou called Jack before responding to Mr. Day. "I've a puzzle for you to solve, along with some interesting information. Which do you want first?"

"Oh, the puzzle of course."

"Okay. Why was Frieda Bowman's body left on the catwalk in Manistee? It seems like that's the last place someone would leave a body."

"I agree. I'll get right on it. What's your information?"

"I received a letter from a man named Joseph Day, in Lima, Ohio who is looking for an Arthur S. Dickenson. He says Webberson is not dead."

"Back to square one."

"Back to square one, if he is right," Lou added. "Need I remind you that I've said that his being alive was always a possibility?"

"I know. Okay Lou, I'll solve your puzzle or at least come up with a theory."

"Thanks."

Lou sent an e-mail to Mr. Day in Lima, Ohio.

Thank you for your note. I would very much like to talk with you. Please call at your convenience.

Lou included both phone numbers, home and cell.

Within a minute of the e-mail being sent, the phone rang in the Searing home. "I'll get it," Lou said to Carol. "I'm hoping it's for me."

"Mr. Searing?"

"Yes."

"This is Joe Day in Lima, Ohio. So, we do have something in common."

"Yes, apparently we do. But, you're not investigating a murder, are you?" Lou asked.

"No, I've been contracted by an attorney to find Arthur S. Dickenson. His daughter by a previous marriage, Alice Dickenson Livernois, wishes to find him."

"I see. And, you have found him?"

"I haven't seen him in person, but I'm sure he is alive."

"How do you know this, if I may ask?"

"My research took me to London, where I learned his son was being cared for in a home. The caretaker told me Arthur had just been there. He also said you had been there previously looking for information about Arthur Webberson, as well."

"That's correct. I asked that caretaker, Mr. Postwaite, to let me know if he learned anything of interest, and he hasn't been in touch."

"I can explain that. He said he misplaced your card and deleted your e-mail, but that he knew you were from Michigan and that you were a private investigator.

"I asked if the name Lou Searing, rang a bell. He said, 'Yes, that's his name'."

"That explains it then. I'm so thankful you visited when you did," Lou replied. "So, Arthur lives!"

"As of yesterday, he lives."

While Lou was talking to Mr. Day, Lou's cell phone recorded a message. Lou returned Jack's call. "Don't tell me you solved the puzzle already."

"I doubt I've solved it, but I have an idea."

"Let me hear it."

"The catwalk is 'above' the pier. I looked up 'pier' in the dictionary to see what was above it on the page, and I saw the word 'pieplant,' which means 'garden rhubarb.' I looked up 'rhubarb,' and, of course, one of the meanings is 'a heated dispute or controversy'."

"And, when was Frieda in a heated dispute? In Bailey's Harbor, Wisconsin."

"BINGO! You're catching on, Lou. And in a dispute with whom? Elmer Edwards, a descendent of the innkeeper on Squaw Island. I think he is our man, Lou."

"Whoa, not so fast, not so fast," Lou countered. "Webberson is reported to be alive, remember."

"OK. Where are you going with this, Lou?" Jack asked.

"Imagine this scenario. Arthur wanted to leave his life in Michigan behind, as he did in Ohio. He called his family together to explain the distribution of his wealth, then devised a plan to feign his death, and used his money and influence to pull it off. He contracted with Jenny to kill Frieda, which implicated Elmer. That led everyone, including us, to believe that Elmer also killed Arthur as revenge for the murder of his grandfather."

"But what about the funeral home?" Jack asked.

"Webberson paid off the funeral home staffers to explain to authorities that the body was dropped off there and then picked up supposedly by the daughter. However, the person who dropped off and picked up the body a couple of days later was Jenny, who used a new vehicle which Arthur had bought her. She wore a hat and sunglasses to partially disguise herself, but the maintenance man, whether he is in on the plot or not, recognized the vehicle because he is interested in buying the same model SUV."

"So, no body was ever left at the funeral home?"

"There never was a body."

"Then the funeral home staff went along with the deception?"

"At least those who were in a position to see the body or deal with the body kept quiet. This also explains why the funeral home didn't respond to the county sheriff, who no doubt asked if the Webberson body was there when the all-points-bulletin was issued."

"So, nobody was put in a body bag or prepared for cremation."

"No, my guess is, 'things' were put in the bag, tagged as 'Arthur S. Webberson' bearing instructions not to do anything with the body."

"Why Jenny, Lou?"

"A college student can always use money, and it being summer, Jenny had time to get caught up in a drama. She knew how to kill Frieda from her class in poisons. She appears strong enough to help someone get a deadweight body up onto a catwalk."

"So, you think she may have talked to Arthur about his brother's intention; and then Arthur actually 'hired' her to work for him in carrying out his plan," Jack concluded.

"Precisely. And, we'll ask Mickey to check the secretary of state's temporary license tags for one issued to Jenny Mitchell or Arthur Webberson, and my guess is that Jenny's name will appear."

"So, if you are right, Arthur used his money to devise and carry out this plan to set up Elmer Edwards as a murderer. Then he could leave the country to be with his mistress in Jolly Old England."

"If I'm right, yes, that's what happened" Lou concluded. "And, one more thing, Jack. The release name was Alice something or other; you said his daughter in Lima is named Alice, and my guess is none of our suspects knew that, but Arthur surely did.

"Hmmm, it makes sense. It's ingenious, and a bit far-fetched, but I suppose it could work. What about the crossword puzzles, Lou?"

"Arthur knows lighthouse history. Jenny knows crossword puzzles. It was a way to tie it all to Elmer."

"But the letters that were left out of crossword puzzles?" Jack asked.

"Yes, they spell revenge, which is appropriate."

"No, they almost spell revenge," Jack corrected. "An E is not accounted for."

"Which means someone else is scheduled to die?" Jack questioned.

"Could be, in which case Jenny needs to be picked up pronto. I'll call Chief McFadden."

Jack brought the case to the obvious conclusion. "Only one thing can give your theory full credibility, and that is to clear Elmer Edwards, because if he figures into this drama in any way, your theory is down the drain."

"You're right, Jack. Let's suggest to Chief McFadden that he get Jenny off the street and then see what Elmer has to say for himself."

Lou called Mickey and explained their conclusions regarding the case. Mickey said he would work with enforcement partners in Ludington and Ann Arbor. "The prosecutor will need you to provide all of your information, and I'm sure you will cooperate."

"Absolutely, we always do, Mickey. Chief, the last thing to do, if I am correct in my solution to this mess, is to get information from Elmer Edwards."

"We'll do that, Lou. We know where he lives, and we'll see what he knows."

"Okay, that that's it from here, Mickey."

"Excellent job, as always, Lou."

"Our pleasure to help. Till next time, Mickey."

"Thank you, Lou, and thanks to Jack as well."

22

OCTOBER 9

Once Arthur Webberson's trial and sentencing was complete, and there was no appeal of the guilty verdict, Lou and Jack were granted permission to meet with Arthur in prison. Jack and Lou found themselves seated across a table from a man, sans monocle, and wearing orange prison garb, who had challenged them and lost.

Arthur began, "I shouldn't have thought I could fool you two. That was my mistake; I should have remembered your friendship with Chief McFadden."

"Thanks for the compliment, I guess," Lou responded. "But we do have some questions, and we hope you are willing to discuss the reasons behind your actions."

"Tell me what you want to know."

Lou began. "What does the string of unfinished words from the crossword puzzles mean?"

"'Never underestimate the power of greed' were Elmer Edwards' words at the Elderhostel conference in Wisconsin. Dr. Wilkenson's speech was videotaped. I thought the authorities would view that tape as part of the investigation of Frieda's death or my death. They would hear Elmer say those words and immediately tie him to the crossword puzzles."

"Wasn't it a risk to frame Elmer without knowing whether he had an alibi for when Frieda was murdered, and for when you supposedly were killed?"

"No, we covered it very well; it wasn't a risk at all. He lives alone and we only needed to find a block of time when no one could vouch for his whereabouts."

"Why was Jenny your accomplice?" Jack asked.

"Jenny approached me to say that Ted wished me dead, which didn't surprise me. I asked her to help me kill Frieda and feign my death. I promised her a lot of money, as well as a vehicle, and convinced her that our plan was foolproof. She went along with it."

"Why did you put Frieda's body up on the catwalk in Manistee? Why not tie her to a cinder block and drop her into the channel?" Lou asked.

"That was part of my playing a word game." Arthur took a deep breath. "The word above 'pier' in the dictionary is 'pieplant' or 'rhubarb', and that was a subtle clue that no one could possibly figure out, but it was to relate to the rhubarb that Elmer had with Frieda." Jack winked at Lou. "It was the middle of the night, and there was no one around and we saw no surveillance cameras. It was pretty easy, and besides, I wanted the body found."

"Was there a connection to the message, 'Never underestimate the power of greed'?" Jack asked.

"Oh sure. Look at everyone connected with the case. They all were caught in the grip of greed."

"As were you," Jack pointed out.

"Probably. I'm human. But, Rose coveted lighthouses, Norman coveted my money. Wally coveted my money, and Victoria wanted even more money. Alice and Arnold are now suing for millions they don't even need. Ted wanted to end my life and secure more of an inheritance. Greed fueled this entire mess."

"Was anyone else supposed to die?" Lou asked. "One word in the sentence wasn't a part of a puzzle on a body."

"No. The plan was to kill only Frieda and then to feign my death."

"How did Frieda die?" Jack asked.

"She agreed to meet me in Manistee the evening of July 2 to discuss some HOMES Lighthouse Association business. Jenny joined us; I told Frieda she was a friend's daughter. After dinner I suggested we take a drive to watch the sunset. I drugged her, and Jenny used her knowledge of poisons to kill her. We waited till three in the morning when the pier was deserted, and then wheeled her out to the light and hauled her up onto the catwalk."

"But, why the funeral home deception?" Jack asked.

"Because I needed to prove that I had died."

"But why send Jenny to the funeral home if there was no body?" Lou asked.

"We thought the deception would seem more real if she went through the motions with the maintenance man. That way he could answer questions as if it had happened."

"So, the funeral home people were paid to keep all of this a secret?" Jack asked.

"Oh yes, money can get me whatever I need or want. We worked through the plan with Mr. Kammeraad, Lisa, and Ken James, and it seemed tight. But Mr. James didn't keep his end of the bargain — guess I didn't pay him enough."

"You left me a message asking me why Dr. Wilkenson began the lecture talking about a murder?"

"Yes, because he knew of the Squaw Island Lighthouse murder. If you had looked into that, you would have learned that the dead keeper was Lawrence Edwards, and that would have steered you to Elmer Edwards. You could then have concluded that Elmer wanted revenge for his grandfather's death, providing him a motive to murder me. The three elements that point to Elmer were the phrase, 'Never underestimate the power of greed', the verbal confrontation with Frieda, and the wish to avenge his grandfather's 1925 death. It was a good plan — a very good plan."

"You know, Mr. Webberson, I still don't get it," Lou admitted. "Why didn't you simply give away your money and go to England? Why did someone have to die, and why did you need to stage an elaborate deception?"

"Family. It was all about family and revenge. The missing letters in the puzzles spelled REVENGE, and all the suspects were vengeful, so the word wasn't intended to be of much assistance in solving the case. My grandfather, Loren Scully, took the gold from his ship, the Sophia Morgan, buried it, and later went back for it, only to find that the keeper had taken it.

"Autumn Angers probably led you to believe that Loren Scully killed Mr. Edwards, but the official report of the murder proves my grandfather was not involved. Lawrence Edwards was murdered by his son, Joseph, who framed my grandfather. Joseph wrote the note in the Bible, not Lawrence. Joseph's mother really saw the shadow of her son and probably recognized his voice when he said, 'He dies because he saw me take the gold.' No doubt she died of depression; after all, she knew her son had killed her husband.

"I framed Elmer Edwards because his family should pay a price for taking the gold that rightfully belonged to my grandfather, Loren Scully.

"So, the Scully family, my ancestors, not only lost the gold that was rightfully ours, but also was wrongfully accused of murder as well. I almost went after the gold when I learned that Ruth Botsford had it in Oregon, but I was sympathetic to her caring for her son. My oldest son has a serious disability, as you know, and cold-hearted as many would consider me to be, I didn't have the heart to hurt her or to take the money she no doubt needed."

"So, you would have had your revenge if Elmer spent the rest of his life in prison?" Lou concluded.

"In my mind, his loss would even the score while I went to England and lived with the only woman I truly love."

"But, now you're the one spending your life in prison," Jack said.

"Yes. Not only did I not even the score, but also the Edwards family continues to cause us pain and frustration."

"In reality, Mr. Webberson, you caused the agony and pain," Lou said. "Forgiveness and letting go of the past would have kept you a free man."

"Well, I have plenty of time to reflect on that. But I thought I could fool you, Mr. Searing."

"Well, you almost did. You simply involved weaker people in your plans. James and Jenny are not good liars. And, having your name on a body bag in the funeral home didn't serve you well, either. It was the call from Two Men and a Truck that turned the case around."

"I know."

"And, your visit to your son's home in London didn't help your cause."

"No, but I sure didn't expect you to go all the way to London to research my history."

"Whatever it takes, right Jack?" Lou remarked looking Jack in the eye.

"Yes, sir. Whatever it takes."

"Thank you for talking with us, Arthur," Lou said sincerely. "You didn't have to share all of this, but it helps us bring closure to those involved."

"You're welcome. Oh, and Mr. Searing, I'd like to ask two favors of you."

"What might they be?"

"My lawyer, William Scott, will be contacting you with a check for two million dollars. I ask you to ensure that Mary McCracken is cared for as long as she lives. She will need someone to see that she gets whatever she needs, and if she dies before the money is gone, put the remainder in a foundation named for my brother Ted to fund respite care for families of people with Alzheimer's or dementia."

"Those are the two favors?" Lou asked.

"No that's just the first. The second is this: I know you're Catholic. Might you ask a priest of your choosing, who in your opinion would be willing to hear my confession and absolve me of my sins, to visit me? That would be a start."

"I will see that Mary is taken care of and I will see that a priest visits you soon."

Arthur rose, took a few steps toward the guard, then turned to face Lou and Jack. He looked each in the eye as if wanting to continue the conversation, but instead lowered his head and slowly shook it from side to side. After a few seconds, Arthur turned and slowly continued to walk toward the guard.

A new chapter in his life was about to begin.

E	P	I	L	O	G	U	E

Arthur Webberson was arrested in New York City as he deplaned a flight from London. He was tried and found guilty of arranging the murder of Frieda Bowman, setting up Elmer Edwards as a murderer, and deceiving authorities. He is serving his sentence in a correctional facility in Ionia, Michigan.

Jenny Mitchell was arrested, tried and found guilty of murdering Frieda Bowman and of acting as an accomplice in deceiving authorities concerning Arthur Webberson. She is serving her sentence in a woman's correctional facility in southeastern Michigan.

Florence Webberson moved to Florida and has a palatial home outside of Palm Beach with an incredible view of the ocean. When told her husband was alive, she admitted knowing about his plans to begin a new life with his mistress in England. She is currently estranged from Wally, but sees Victoria and her family once a year.

Andrew Webberson plays concerts all over Europe and the money he earns is held by a trust with plans to build a performing arts center for musicians with disabilities.

Wally Webberson and his wife Bea divorced. Wally, homeless, was last seen eating in a soup kitchen in downtown Detroit.

Victoria Webberson Wilkshire and her husband Bertrand remain in Bloomfield Hills, Michigan. Victoria attends weekly sessions with her psychiatrist.

Elmer Edwards was determined to be an innocent player in the drama. Working through his attorney, he was able to cash in the gold at its market value of just under 5 million dollars.

Ruth Botsford willed her share of the gold to an endowment to assure respite care for parents of persons with disabilities

Rose McCracken moved to Saugatuck and operates a very comfortable Lighthouse Bed and Breakfast.

Mary McCracken remained with the Bates and continued to work part-time at Alma College while enjoying her friends at the Gratiot County CAC Center. She forgave Rose and sees her on occasion, but their relationship is fractured.

Ted Webberson died of a massive stroke prior to Arthur's trial. Jenny Mitchell paid his funeral expenses. He was buried in a casket fit for a king. Ike presented the eulogy.

Alice Dickenson Livernois paid her attorney's fees for finding her father. She and her brother Arnold plan to sue their father for back support for her mother and themselves. She is expected to be awarded millions.

Mrs. Bell, Ms. Scheiern and students received a hero's welcome in Greenville, including a parade down Main Street. They were guests on the Today Show and enjoyed their trip to New York. Oh, yes. The treasure chest was opened and contained nothing of value.

J.W. Kammeraad was arrested for fraud. He accepted a plea agreement. However, he lost his mortuary license and planned to sell his state-of-the-art funeral home.

Kenneth James was in on the deception and admitted there never was a body. He explained that he was overcome with guilt, but tried to help Lou without admitting to the truth. He was not charged with any crime.

The HOMES Lighthouse Association is still waiting for Arthur to die to collect their millions. With the estate idle, pending litigation, the board doesn't expect to receive a dime.

Jack Kelly thanked his employer for allowing him time to seize the opportunity of working with Lou Searing. He awaits a call from Lou to become involved in solving another murder. Lou promised to call.

Lou and Carol, Samm and Millie decided to slow down a bit and enjoy their home on the shore of Lake Michigan. Carol spends time in her quilting studio, and Lou is penning a new novel which would be titled, *The Lighthouse Murders*. In the evening they walk along the shore of Lake Michigan, hand in hand, enjoying sunsets and each other.

To order additional copies of The Lighthouse Murders, as well as other mysteries, please go to www.buttonwoodpress. com and follow directions. If you wish to contact the author, please e-mail him at RLBald@aol.com.